Kaine Agary grew up in Port Harcourt, Nigeria. She has lived in the United States of America and now lives in Lagos, Nigeria, where she is the Editor of *TAKAii* magazine. This is her first work of fiction.

Yellow-Yellow

A NOVEL BY KAINE AGARY

Dtalkshop
Lagos

A Dtalkshop Paperback
Published in Nigeria by Dtalkshop
26 Commercial Avenue, P.O. Box 3183
Sabo, Yaba, Lagos
Email: info@dtalkshop.com
http://www.dtalkshop.com

ISBN: 978-070-833-2

For my grandparents
Chief and Mrs. R. J. E. Koripamo

One

During my second to last year in secondary school, one of the crude oil pipes that ran through my village broke and spilled oil over several hectares of land, my mother's farm included. I was at home that day when she returned shortly after leaving for the farm. When she got to the house, she knocked on the door and said very coolly, "Zilayefa, bring me my bathing soap and sponge." As I was wondering why she needed them, I saw that her legs were stained black.

"What happened?" I asked.

"And bring my towel too," she said, ignoring my question.

"What happened?" There was more urgency in my voice as I touched her and looked over every part of her body. My heart was pounding against my chest as I tried to imagine what could have happened that left her void of words. My mother never fought, and she did not look like she was injured in any way, but when she was upset, she got very quiet.

"Oil, Zilayefa," she said, and turned away from me, walking towards the river. My mother hardly ever called me Zilayefa; she called me Yellow-Yellow, like everybody else.

"Oil? From where?" I was walking behind her, and then I heard people shouting.

A group of people, painted in the same black as my mother, some covered from head to toe, was marching to see the Amananaowei, the head of the village. I joined them to find out what had happened. It turned out some of them had also lost their farmland that day. They were marching to the Amananaowei's house to report the matter and demand that he take it up with the oil company. Some were crying; others were talking about compensation.

I left them and ran to my mother's farm. It was the first time I saw what crude oil looked like. I watched as the thick liquid spread out, covering more land and drowning small animals in its path. It just kept spreading and I wondered if it would stop, when it would stop, how far it would spread. Then there was the smell. I can't describe it but it was strong—so strong it made my head hurt and turned my stomach. I bent over, and retched so hard I became dizzy. It felt like everything had turned to black and was spinning around me. There was so much oil, and we could do nothing with it—viscous oil that would not dry out, black oil that was knee-deep. I stayed there, in a daze, until someone shouted at me, "You no go commot for there? You dey look like say na beta tin'! Come on, leave dat place!"

The community took the matter up with the oil company that owned the pipes, but they said they suspected sabotage by the youths and were not going to pay compensation for all the destruction that the burst pipes had caused. And so it was that, in a single day, my mother lost her main source of sustenance. However, I think she had lost that land a long time ago, because each season yielded less than the season before. Not unlike the way she and others in the village had gradually lost, year after year, the creatures of the river to oil spills, acid rain, gas flares, and who knows what else, according to the voices on the radio.

Two

"Yellow-Yellow." That is what most people in my village called me because of my complexion, the product of a Greek father and an Ijaw mother. My father was a sailor whose ship had docked briefly in Nigeria about one year before I was born. After months at sea, he was just happy to see a woman and would have told her anything to have her company. The woman he chose was my mother, a young and naïve eighteen-year-old who had just moved to Port Harcourt from her small village with visions of instant prosperity. She had completed her secondary-school education and had passed her school-leaving examinations. With that qualification, she hoped to get a good job in Port Harcourt. After all, Nigeria was in the middle of the oil boom, and there were many businessmen around. She saw herself working as a secretary for one of them. Instead, she met my father at a disco and fell for him.

For the few weeks that he was in Port Harcourt, she was in heaven. She believed that she had found her life partner and that this man would take care of her. I don't think my father ever told her that he would marry her; she just assumed that he would. Instead, he left Port Harcourt without saying good-bye. She went to the port to look for him one day, as had become her habit, and was told that his ship had left. There was no message; he was just gone, leaving behind his planted seed in my mother's *belle*.

Disillusioned, my mother went back to her village to face the shame of being an unwed mother with nothing but dreams about my future. She would make sure that I accomplished what she had not. She had inherited a small piece of land from her family, which she farmed, and sometimes she would go fishing. With the proceeds, she was able to feed us and pay my school fees. She took care of all my needs and even went without sometimes to make sure that I got an education. For instance, she expelled herself from the women's group so that she would not be forced to spend money on wrappers for their outings.

I think it was for a festival in another village that the women's group had distributed the uniform wrapper to all their members. One month later, when the chairlady came to collect my mother's payment, my mother brought the wrapper out from where it had been lying in her bedroom from the day it entered our house and handed it over to her.

"Na de money I come to collect o," the chairlady said, trying not to sound irritated.

"I no get money so I dey return de cloth. I neva cut am," my mother responded coldly.

"Bibi, na wa for you o. We all poor but we dey join hand help each other. De day wey you go need something, make you no come meet us o," the chairlady threatened.

"I hear. I no join dis una women group again sef. I neva see any beta tin wey come out of am. Dey go!" My mother, still very detached, showed the chairlady out.

When the chairlady left, she sighed to herself, "I don't even see what they do with the dues they collect. Better for me to save my money!" That was the end of women's group activities for my mother and the beginning of her self-expulsion from all social groups.

My mother used to tell me that I would be better than her, that, as long as I was educated, I would be able to take care of myself. I did not question her. She said it with such conviction and made so many sacrifices to make sure that I went to school that I believed it to be true.

I did well in school. Compared to my classmates, I was above average. We did not have all the textbooks, because most of us could not afford them, and the school could barely afford to pay teachers, much less provide books. So, we relied entirely on taking copious notes during lectures, in addition to the notes that our teachers handed out to us. Since school was the only thing I had to worry about, it was not difficult keeping up with my schoolwork. Unlike other parents who kept their children busy, my mother would not allow me to do too many chores around the house or follow her into the bush for firewood and for the other things that people went into the bush for. It was almost as though she was obsessed, consumed by the idea that my education would save me from what I had yet to understand and what she could not explain to me. Perchance in saving me, she hoped to save herself.

* * *

Sometimes, when I would sit outside with boys and girls in my age group, we would listen to the radio, and sometimes we would hear an Ijaw person, living in Port Harcourt or Lagos, speaking about how the oil companies had destroyed our Niger Delta with impunity. They would discuss how the Ijaws and other ethnic groups were suffering and even dying while the wealth of their soil fed others. They would proffer ideas about what the oil companies and the government had to do.

These broadcasts drove the boys in my village to violence. If we had to suffer amidst such plenty, then these boys would cause as much havoc as possible until someone took interest in our plight and until justice, as they saw it, prevailed. Some of them joined the boys from other villages to kidnap oil company executives or bar oil company workers from doing their work. Mostly they were successful, but sometimes one or two of our boys failed to return from a mission. The word around the village was that the police had caught and killed them, but we would not hear about this on the radio.

Usually we did not get good reception on the radio, so we would play *awigiri* tapes and dance, but I had to be careful that my mother did not catch me. "Dance your whole brain away if you like," she would say. She disliked me "wasting" my time; especially when there were better things to do like plan my entry into a university. In her dreams, I would go on to university and study a subject that would get me a good job with enough income to take care of myself. If I could take care of myself, then I could take care of her. She did not say this, but I knew what was expected of me: I was her only child, and she had made so many sacrifices for me. For this, I knew that if I did not take care of her when I could finally take care of myself, the spirits of the water would tie my womb and make sure that, for my ungratefulness, I never experienced the joy of motherhood.

The day my mother's farmland was overrun by crude oil was the day her dream for me started to wither, but she carried on watering it with hope. The black oil that spilled that day swallowed my mother's crops and unravelled the threads that held together her fantasies for me. She was able to find new farmland in another village, but it was not the same. Some who owned land they were not using would allow others to farm on it until they needed to use it. My mother got one such piece of land. She rowed her canoe there and back every day with unwavering determination. In her mind, she would find a way to make sure I completed my education. I did not care as much as she did about finishing school; I just wanted to leave the village. The sameness of life in the village would kill me if I did not escape.

All my life, I had always had something to do. Always had something planned for me by my mother. By the time I finished school, my mother did not have enough money for university. I could not even take the qualifying examinations because she did not have the registration fee. She promised herself that she would find it in time for the next year; after that, all she thought and spoke about was how to find the money for my schooling.

On one of those rare occasions that we got good reception on the radio, we heard that the oil companies had educational scholarships for Niger Delta indigenes. The problem was that we never got more information after that announcement. Nobody told us where we could go to apply for them. Nobody told us what exactly we needed in order to qualify for one. Somewhere out there were marvellous scholarships from the oil companies, but they were useless to us because no one in my village knew how to get them. None of this mattered much to me. I was as interested in these scholarships as I was in finishing school, but my mother saw this as a way to achieve her dream of my success.

Three

"*Ere ow'ama bien mo gbein mo daba, owei mo 'yaimo aki, hm hm.*" Robert Ebizimor's voice blared from the radio sitting on the front window of Mama Ebiye's house. The young people in my age group had taken up her frontage, dancing as Robert instructed us girls to throw our backsides and the boys to pick them up. We were having so much fun until I heard my mother's stern voice behind me: "Yellow!"

After finishing my housework that day, I had gone over to Mama Ebiye's house to kill time until my mother got back from her farm. Some of us had just finished our final examinations and were excited about achieving even that, not sure what was ahead of us. Mama Ebiye had bought us some bottles of soft drinks that we girls shared among ourselves; the boys had come with two bottles of shine-your-eye, which I also partook of, although I could not drink too much because sometimes the mix of alcohol and roots cramped my stomach. Mama Ebiye was excited that Ebiye, her last child, had finished secondary school and was, hopefully, on his way to being the first graduate in the family.

"Bibi, *tubara?* How farm today?" Mama Ebiye asked jovially as she walked over to my mother.

"Not bad," my mother responded, with her eyes on me.

I knew I was in trouble; that was the end of my celebration! A heart-tugging lecture was sure to follow as soon as my mother got me alone inside our house.

"The children don endure, finish school, so I dey celebrate for dem," Mama Ebiye offered excitedly.

My mother did not respond. Her eyes were fixed on me. I knew I was expected to scamper home, but I didn't, hoping that Mama Ebiye would save me and that I could continue in the celebration.

"Bibi, school don finish! Make Yellow enjoy herself. Even professor dem dey rest," Mama Ebiye teased as she pulled my mother away from the party and led her to our house.

Nobody was closer to my mother than Mama Ebiye, but they quarrelled a lot. The good thing was that their quarrels never lasted for more than a few hours, so Mama Ebiye's house was never off-limits to me. Her house was the only one from which my mother allowed me to eat. "The world is bad," my mother would say. "You don't know what someone has put in the food they offer you."

Mama Ebiye had four sons, no daughters, so she spoiled all the girls she liked. She would buy us little gifts, like hair accessories or underwear, when she went to Port Harcourt to buy stock for her shop or to visit her sons.

As Mama Ebiye led my mother away, I heard her say, "Yellow no be small pickin again o. You go allow de girl grow o. After all na inside house you siddon born de pickin?"

Later that evening, after everyone had dispersed, I was afraid to go home because I knew that, though my mother had given in to Mama Ebiye and left me to continue throwing my backside for the boys to pick up, I was sure to hear how stupid I had been for "forgetting myself."

I walked into the house as quietly as possible, hoping to put off the inevitable for as long as I could. I was even willing to forego whatever my mother had cooked for supper that night just so I would avoid the scolding. As I was approaching the safety of my bedroom, it came.

"Yellow-Yellow, so you don't have anything better to do than to *gbein mo* your backside like a jobless girl?" My mother's voice was calm. I waited for more words to follow, but she didn't say anything more. To be on the safe side, I went straight to my room and stayed there until I fell asleep. From then until the day I left my village, I tried to occupy my time with activities that my mother approved of. Dancing in public was certainly not one of them.

* * *

One day, almost a year after I finished secondary school, I came up with my master escape plan from the village. I decided I would have to find someone to take me away. It would have to be during one of those celebrations where many people came in from the city: maybe a burial, a wedding, or a chieftaincy installation. Because such events created a lot of excitement in the village, I figured it would be easy to slip away from my mother's watchful eyes and meet that special someone who would save me from certain death in my claustrophobic village.

Shortly after I had made this decision, Mama Ebiye took me on a trip to Port Harcourt. We went to a bend-down boutique where I bought second-hand dresses in which I intended to execute my plan of action. I had saved some money from *dashes* I got during Christmas and other times when out-of-towners came to visit, but I discovered that my money was not worth as much as I had hoped. Still, I was able to buy some simple, inexpensive dresses, and I was happy with my choices. My favourite was made of light powder-blue jersey fabric with floral designs. The dress had cap sleeves and a small-cup bodice that encased my breasts, while the rest of the dress clung gently to my torso and flared over my hips before swinging softly to mid-calf. I liked how the bodice caressed my breasts and the way the skirt brushed my hips when I walked. I felt good, especially because the dress would not raise any suspicions from my mother, or so I thought. I did not want anyone to know of my plans, especially my mother. I could not allow myself to think about how she would react if she found out.

A few days later, providence came calling when I overheard my mother telling another neighbour, Mama Tonye, that the funeral rites of Chief Semoke, who had died in Lagos a month earlier, were coming up next month. Chief Semoke was from our village, but he didn't visit much, even with the renown of his family name in the village. He and his brothers had built a big, two-storey house eight years earlier when their father died. Since then, however, neither he nor his family members visited the village. When his father died, Chief Semoke, his brothers, and their many friends from the city descended upon the village. I hoped the same friends, and perhaps more, would show up at his burial ceremony.

The week before the burial, people started arriving at the Semoke family house. My friend Priye and I went over there to talk to them and discovered that some of them were there just to cook during the period. We asked one of the women who was there to cook if we could help them serve food and drinks. She did not see a problem, so we agreed that we would go back to the house when the Semoke family arrived and they would give us more instructions then. Providence was still in town, and I was counting the hours before I would ride out of the village with my saviour.

The Semoke family arrived that Friday, and the family invited people to view the body, holding a wake that lasted all night. As tradition dictated, Chief Semoke's first child danced around the crowd with a picture of Chief Semoke. It was the first time I got a close look at Chief Semoke's face. Before that, I had been unable to summon up the courage to go into the room where the chief's body lay in a white casket. However, after seeing his photograph, I was less afraid, and thus, swallowing hard, I entered the room. He looked grey and old, nothing like his picture. His face looked very peaceful, yet it was not the peace of sleep.

The next day was the church service, followed by the interment. After that, we served special guests from out of town in a private room where we had set up the food buffet-style so that they could help themselves. There was *kekefia*, *banga* soup, pepper soup, *jollof* rice, coconut rice, prawns roasted in banana leaves, meat stew, and a very colourful fruit bowl. There was usually a lot of food at funerals, especially if the family was rich, and most villagers attended these funerals solely for the food, drinks, and music. Three years earlier, at Chief Tariye's funeral ceremony, a man was found curled up in a corner outside the house, lying dead in his own vomit. He had gorged himself with food and *kainkain* for two days.

After everyone sat down, I stood close to the door and informed them what we were serving for lunch. Afterwards, I went to each individual to take drink orders. While I was talking, I noticed a man across the room. I don't know how I missed him before, because his complexion stood out just as mine did in that room. His skin was the colour of ripe plantain peel. His hair was black and had the same big waves as my own. I had been staring at him for much longer than was comfortable, so he smiled at me and I smiled back. I wondered if he was Greek. The similarities in our physical attributes reminded me how different I was from everyone else in the village.

I cannot say that I ever really longed for my father; in fact, I barely thought of him at all. My mother hardly spoke about him. I had learnt not to ask questions, because each time I did, she very tactfully dodged them, changed the subject, or she would ask, "Have I not taken good care of you? Why are you asking of your father?" I did not care for him one way or another, but seeing this man brought me thoughts of my father. Where was he? Did he ever come back to Nigeria? Did he ever think of my mother? Would I know him if I saw him? I had no clue what my father looked like. My mother had no pictures of him, and it did not help that, aside from my complexion, I looked just like her, right down to the little birthmark below her left eye. When I looked at her, I saw a petite woman with an oval face, big dreamy eyes, a nose that looked like God was running low on clay the day he made it, and small lips that parted to reveal a charming gap-toothed smile. People often said to me, "Your mother just went and gave birth to her twin."

I came back with a crate of drinks and placed the bottles on the table so that people could pick what they wanted. As I opened drinks for some of the other guests, I noticed that the mystery man had picked a club soda. When I got to him, he was engrossed in a conversation, so I lingered a little as I opened his drink and poured it into his glass. If I got his attention, then maybe he would be at least a little curious about me. I hoped. I prayed. As I put down the half-empty bottle, he turned and looked up at me. He smiled his thanks, and I smiled back, ecstatic.

About a half hour after I had served refreshments, he came out of the private room with an empty bottle in his hand and stopped to talk to one of the cooks. I saw her point him in my direction, so I walked towards him. As I got closer to him, he raised his bottle and smiled. I felt the blood rush to my head as I quickly looked down shyly. I stood half-facing him so that he could not see how red my face had become. When he asked me my name, I responded, "Zilayefa." He looked a little confused, so I added, "You can call me Laye."

"Nice name. What does it mean?" he asked.

"There is nothing like giving birth to a child," I rolled off my tongue in what I thought was a sophisticated accent.

He cracked a smile and responded, "Nice. My name is Sergio."

I liked the sound of his voice; he spoke in a monotone that would normally irritate me, but his accent and the softness in his voice put me at ease. I reached out to take the bottle from him and asked if he wanted another. When he said yes, I quickly went to get it. For me this was a good sign: He did not have to come out of the room to get another drink, but he did. He could have asked anyone else, but he did not. At that point, I knew I had gotten his attention. I did not have to do much more. In my juvenile mind, I thought he would come to me and fall desperately in love with me and rescue me from my colourless existence.

On Sunday, the Semoke family had a thanksgiving service at St. Stephen's Anglican Church. Many of their out-of-town guests had left after lunch the day before, but Sergio was still in town and attended the church service with the family.

After the service, I walked up behind him and said, "Good morning, Sergio," as I passed him and kept walking. I wondered how long he was staying in the village. I had overheard one of the cooks saying that Chief Semoke's brother and his friend would be around until the end of the week. I hoped that the friend they were referring to was Sergio. Armed with that hope, I kept walking because I knew, in my heart of hearts, I would see him again.

Sunday evenings were always quiet in my village, and that evening was no exception. I was sitting on the porch outside my mother's house, enjoying the evening air, when I saw Sergio strolling down the path that passed the house.

As he came closer, I got up from my seat and walked up to him. "Where are you going?" I asked him after bidding him good evening.

"Nowhere. I am just taking a walk. Exploring a little and enjoying the serene atmosphere," he replied, and paused a little. "Would you like to join me?"

I gave him a little nod, and we started walking together without speaking. My mother's house was close to the riverbank, away from the centre of the village, so we walked towards the river. We found a spot about two hundred metres away from the house and sat under a tree to watch the sun set. We could still see the orange sun, fading away into the sky, through the layer of smoke from gas flares in the neighbouring villages.

We sat in silence for what seemed like an hour until I asked him why he was still in the village. He said he was with his friend Tarilabo, Chief Semoke's younger brother, and that they were trying to conduct some business. They were interested in logging timber from the forests in our village and wanted to discuss that possibility with the Amananaowei.

It turned out that Sergio was an antique-furniture dealer from Spain who travelled extensively for his business and had met Tarilabo on one of his trips to London five years earlier. They had struck up a friendship almost immediately and had gone into business together soon after. His antique business was beginning to bore him, and he wanted to try something new. For this reason, he had come to Nigeria to further investigate a business proposition of Tarilabo's. I was so awed by his worldly business talk, all I could think to say was, "Good luck."

We were very engrossed in our conversation, with him doing most of the talking, that I barely noticed it had gotten dark. I looked behind us, towards the village, and all was pitch-black. Some boys were suspected to have stolen and sold the transformer for the village generator, so there was no electricity. Only people like the Amananaowei, the local government chairman, and other wealthy people such as the Semokes could afford a household generator. For the rest of us, even when the village generator was working, there was always conflict about where the funds for diesel would come from, especially since some other local governments managed to provide the luxury of a standby generator at no cost to their constituents.

I got up and told Sergio that it was time to head back into the village. He agreed and said that he and Tarilabo were going into the forest the next day but that he had really enjoyed sitting and talking with me. So, if I did not have anything planned, he would like to see me after they got back from the forest. I told him I would really like that, and we parted outside my mother's house.

I had thought that when I met my someone special, I would feel butterflies in my stomach, lose touch with reality, and we would be riding together into the sunset. None of that had happened, but I was comfortable with him, and I enjoyed the sound of his voice—so much that sometimes I concentrated more on it than on what he said. But at this point, that was it. I was not in love, not that I had any idea what love would feel like. I had expected that when love, or something close to it, hit me, it would be like a rough current against a canoe; somewhat like what I was sure my mother had felt with my father, if that was love. But love was not my desire—I simply wanted a way out of the village, and if love came with escape, it would be a bonus.

The next evening, Sergio came by my mother's house to meet me. He was wearing khaki shorts with a white polo shirt and khaki shoes, which, he told me, were called *espadrilles*. He was about five feet, ten inches tall, with the body of a football player—very strong, with slightly bowed legs and thick ankles. His calves were well defined; as we used to say in secondary school, he had yams for legs, perfectly *yamulous* legs. His chest was broad, and his stomach, though not firm, did not hang over his belt. His small, hazel eyes stayed hidden behind very long, dark eyelashes, and his arched brows were dark and thick. Although he had a few streaks of grey hairs on the sides of his head, he did not look half bad. If I had to guess his age, I would have put him between forty-five and fifty.

My mother greeted him cordially and then said to me in Ijaw, "Don't go and get carried away and spoil yourself o. My back is not ready for grandchildren." Sergio asked me later what she had said. I lied and told him she had only reminded me not to stay out too late.

I had some ripening plantain and iced fish that I had put in a pepper sauce for a few hours. I also had two coconuts that had fallen from the tree in my mother's backyard a few days before. I put the plantain, fish, and coconut, along with a small jar of palm oil, into a basket and covered the basket with plantain leaves.

As I stepped out with the basket, Sergio took it from me and asked what was in it. I looked at him flirtatiously, without answering, but firmly placed my hand over his as he tried to raise the plantain leaves. He looked at me, with one eyebrow raised and a crooked smile, and, for some reason, that excited me. I was taking him to one of my favourite spots—a small uninhabited island about five hundred meters away from my side of the village. My friends and I called the island *Wokiri*, our land, because it was the only place where we could do whatever we wanted without the adults disturbing us.

When we reached the riverbank, I untied my mother's canoe; Sergio placed the basket in the canoe and helped me push it into the river. Even though he kept asking to paddle on our way to Wokiri, I insisted on doing it myself, promising him I would think about letting him paddle back from the island.

We got to the island, and I tied the canoe to a tree while Sergio carried out all the things I had packed. I led the way to a little area that my friends and I had carved out for ourselves. It had nothing but a small charcoal grill—an old one from my mother's kitchen—a machete, and a bottle of kerosene and matches in a plastic rice bag buried in a hole. That was all we needed since we only grilled fish and plantain and, if we were lucky enough to catch any, shrimp from the traps around the island. After stuffing our stomachs, we would devour coconuts to quench our thirst, and then we would swim. It was our escape from the village—from the conflicts, the violence, and the depression that characterised our village more and more.

I laid out a large wrapper for Sergio and started a fire in the grill. As I sat next to him, he asked me again, "Aren't you going to tell me what is in the basket?"

"Just be patient. You'll see in a minute. As soon as the charcoal burns a little, you'll see," I told him excitedly, hoping that he would enjoy the simple meal I had planned for him.

He arranged himself on the wrapper, lying on his side with his arm propping him up. "Well, it doesn't matter, as long as it doesn't kill me."

"It definitely won't kill you, trust me."

I got up, took the fish and the plantains from the basket, and placed them on the grill. I then cut some banana leaves and put them into the basket in anticipation of the grilled fish and plantain. Sergio watched me in fascination. I was wearing my powder-blue dress, and the evening air brushed my face and whispered through my clothes. The air moving freely through my dress and caressing my body underneath was intoxicating.

I lay next to him as we waited for the food to cook. He asked me questions about myself, and I explained how I had never known my father, a sailor with whom my mother had had a brief affair. I told him that my mother was my only parent, as far as I was concerned, and that we got along very well. My mother's parents had died when she was young, and she had no brothers or sisters, so, basically, my mother was my only family. I lied and told him that I planned on going to university to study business, even though in my heart I knew that I was not very keen on attending university.

I put the plantains and the fish on the banana leaves and poured on some palm oil. I broke the plantains into little pieces and showed Sergio how to pick a piece of plantain, cut a morsel of fish into the plantain, and dip it into the palm oil, all with one hand. I put the first piece in his mouth, and after one or two chomps, his eyes popped open, his face turned red, and he stopped chewing. The pepper from the fish was too hot for him; only then did I realize that I had not carried any drinking water.

I quickly picked up the machete and broke open one of the coconuts so that he could drink the coconut water.

"Are you okay?" I was deeply concerned.

He nodded his head vigorously in a vain attempt to convince me.

"I'm so sorry. I didn't realize it would be too peppery for you."

He swallowed hard, and between moments of sucking in air to cool his sensitive palate, he managed to form the words, "Don't worry. I am okay. It was just a shock to my taste buds. I like it."

As we ate, he kept sucking in air to cool off the burning sensation in his mouth. With one hand, he clamped his nostrils with his fingers to control the dripping from his nose, and with the other, he continued eating. I cracked open the second coconut for him, and he offered me some coconut water before he finished it. He kept eating until the last morsel of fish was gone. He seemed very pleased with himself for finishing the food.

"How are you?" I asked after he had swallowed the last piece of fish and plantain.

"I think I'll feel better after I kiss you." I turned my head to look up at him quizzically and he continued. "Seriously, I think it will help cool the temperature in my mouth."

I laughed, but I obliged—after all, I did not want this white man dying on my hands, and, truthfully, I was beginning to feel butterflies in my stomach. His lips were soft and full, not what I expected with a white person. Teachers in elementary school social studies class taught us that Africans had thick, full lips while whites had thin lips.

Sergio's usually pink lips were now the colour of red hibiscus, and though the kiss was short, I liked it. It wasn't the same as when one of my classmates had kissed me in primary school. A group of us had been playing during break, and the boys started a game where they would pick a girl and kiss her. The boy who kissed me was a nice boy, but it was a horrible kiss, and we never talked about it afterwards. Sergio had not tried to swallow my face or push his tongue down my throat, and he did not insist when I stopped his hand from exploring under the skirt of my dress. I closed my eyes and allowed the feeling from the kiss to linger as we both lay down on my wrapper; he pulled me close and placed my head on his chest. We listened to the river, the trees, the birds, and to each other's breathing, and we talked about the river, the trees, the birds, the land, and all that came from it.

I hoped the night wouldn't end, but all too soon it was time to return home, as my mom would soon start to worry. It had gotten very dark, and I did not trust that Sergio could protect me if we encountered any night creatures. Even though I grew up in the village, my mother had been very protective of me. Consequently, there were many things about bush survival that I did not know and did not think I wanted to experience just then. I allowed Sergio to paddle back to the village, and we left each other with a promise to meet the next day. It would have to be later in the day because he and Tarilabo had planned to go out and survey the potential of the area in which they were interested.

By the time I got home, my mother was in bed, but she was not sleeping, so I got into her bed and snuggled next to her. She asked how my night went, and I responded simply, "Fine." She took a deep breath and did not ask any other questions. I knew that my association with Sergio disturbed her, but she had decided, for whatever reason, not to make a big deal about it.

The next day, I kept myself busy with housework. My mother was out all day, and by the time she came back, I had made her a welcoming pot of *kekefia* and even turned some *osun* for her. We ate together and talked about everything under the sun but Sergio: She was avoiding the subject, and I was not willing to bring it up. Not yet. As time passed, we listened to some recorded music, played a few rounds of *eki okoto,* and after trouncing me severally, she said she was tired and retired to her bedroom.

I waited for Sergio in the living room, as he had said he would be late. I soon dozed off, and when I woke up, it was almost midnight. My chest tightened from fear that Sergio would not come. I tried to take long deep breaths, hoping that I would feel better, and I told myself he would still come that night. He was not a Greek sailor. He was Sergio, the man who I had taken to my special hideaway, the man who had kissed me so tenderly and made me feel butterflies in my stomach, the man whose voice mesmerised me, the one who was my ticket out of the village.

Suddenly my mother was tapping my shoulder to wake me up. I had dozed off again. I looked at my watch; it was three in the morning. I got up and felt as if my insides were being sucked out of me. I wanted to cry, but I was too numb. My rising hopes had been cruelly dashed. I went to my room and climbed into my bed, enveloped by desolation. All I could do was pull my knees up to my chin and lie there, in the foetal position. My mother put a wrapper over me and lay down beside me; she held me tight and did not say a word.

Four

Before my encounter with Sergio, my life had been without direction. I did not know what I wanted to do, and I did not care, either. Up to that point, I had spent my life living my mother's dream that I gain admission into the university and become a "graduate." It did not matter that I had no clue what I wanted to study. Not that it would have mattered, because the universities, if any were interested in me, would decide what I was going to study, based on the results of my examination. I had managed to pass all my subjects with my best scores being in English and English literature.

In school, I had spent much of my time reading books that Mr. Diseye lent me. He had lived in Ghana for many years, teaching at a secondary school until he retired and returned to Nigeria. He came back with all his literature books, a lot of which turned out to be our required reading during my last two years in school. However, that was not why I read. I read because the books took me to other worlds and made me forget my own reality. I knew every square inch of my village, and I felt like a trapped animal. Mr. Diseye demanded only that you handle his books with great care, so I was careful not to put any marks in them or fold the top corners of the pages into little flaps, which he called *elephant ears*. Once I had proved to him that I could treat his books with the attentiveness of a first-time mother to her newborn child, he willingly gave me the vessels that took me into new villages and faraway cities.

Mr. Diseye was highly regarded by everyone. The rumour around the village was that he had been married in Ghana and had two grown sons. However, he had returned to the village alone, and since then, tongues had not stopped wagging about why that was. Some people claimed that his wife, who they maintain was at least fifteen years younger than him, had left him for another man and so, heartbroken, he had returned to Nigeria. I thought it was because he wanted to die and be buried on his own land, as he often said it was important that his bones found their final resting place on the land that gave birth to him.

Sometimes I would visit just to keep him company. We talked about the books I had read, about school, and about the importance of "*educashen.*" He often asked me what I wanted to study in the university, and I could never give him an answer with certainty. He always encouraged me to study English and suggested that I could be a teacher as he had been.

It would have been difficult to know what course to study in the university. Some students who had dreams of becoming medical doctors ended up sullen and depressed, studying pharmacy or microbiology when their examination marks fell short of the cut-off mark required for their dream course. Others with dreams of becoming engineers came out with degrees in architecture or even English! There just were not enough spots in each university to meet the demands of prospective students each year. That was the way things were.

After four or five years in the university, which were peppered with teachers' strikes, student demonstrations, and shutdowns, these students emerged with bachelor's degrees that they would use only for the one year of mandatory National Youth Service Corps as teachers in a rural school. After that, they would end up in banks; marching the halls of government agencies looking for government contracts; or, if they were lucky, they would land a cushy job in an oil company. The oil companies held the pot of gold for all graduates. Most of them provided health care services to their employees through their own hospitals, so doctors were on their payroll. It seemed the oil companies could find a place for every degree—lawyers, administrators, geographers, and engineers were required; all other disciplines fed the nontechnical units, including community relations.

The story was always the same: a few marks short of the cut-off point and your life choices became severely limited. Either you waited another year or two or three to resit the examinations and make the required marks, or you let your existing grades decide where and how you would spend four, five, or six years of your youth. The number of years you spent depended on the consistency of staff salaries, political stability, and student conflicts on campus.

There were those who paid others to sit their examination and successfully went to university to pursue their dreams. Some who took that route had to continue paying people to sit their examinations, and if they were lucky, they received their degrees without being detected. The unlucky ones had their entrance scores questioned on the whim of an overzealous university administrator and faced expulsion, sometimes just one session short of completing their less-than-mediocre ride through the course.

Some young men and women had added pressure from lecturers and professors who wanted to exchange sexual favours for passing grades. An adamant professor could hold students back from graduating for a year or two or until the students gave in to their demands or gathered enough evidence to prove that they were being harassed.

I sometimes thought that this *okoso* system was good for people like me who were not passionate about any particular subject. Our scores would throw us into the race and force direction on those of us who needed to move on but who had not decided where we were headed. I needed to go somewhere, do something besides the daily chores of village life that threatened to choke me to death.

In my graduating class, I was one of five girls in a class of twenty-four students who took the final examinations. The school year had started out with twelve girls and thirty boys in my class, but some of the boys dropped out to take on responsibility for their families. Others dropped out to join the growing army who claimed they were fighting for justice for the Niger Delta.

It was the year after the government hanged Ken Saro-Wiwa, along with nine other Ogonis, for inciting an insurrection, that led to the deaths of four elders in Ogoni land. Every young boy had visions of dying valiantly for the cause, as Ken Saro-Wiwa just had and as Isaac Adaka Boro had done nearly thirty years before him. The reports were that Ken Saro-Wiwa's last words on the day of his execution were, "Lord, take my soul, but the struggle continues." So boys wandered about the village aimlessly, dropping the phrase "*Aluta continua*" at the slightest provocation. As for the girls, they dropped out to have their babies or, as my mother would say, to "turn *ofogorious* with the jobless boys in town."

Considering all these, I decided that an out-of-towner would be my ticket out of my desperate existence, until Sergio's unceremonious exit forced me into a dungeon of tortured soul-searching. Nothing brought me joy. I had so desperately believed that he would take me away with him, because that was part of the perfect scenario woven in my dreams. My head was crammed with thoughts of how I would make it to a city—Port Harcourt, Lagos, anywhere! I went about my daily business with robotic precision. One hundred and fourteen steps, yes, one hundred and fourteen steps was how long it took me to walk from my mother's house to the river. Thirty-four steps took me to Mama Tari's house to buy kerosene. Moreover, most days, one hundred and sixty-seven paddle strokes pulled my canoe to Wokiri.

My thoughts would have my heart thumping with anxiety, as if I had been entwined in fishing net and thrown into the murky waters of the River Nun; each movement, each attempted breath, forced me down to a lifeless state at the bottom of the river. I had to come up with something to do to stay alive. I started to consider options that had never crossed my mind before, and from what I knew of my mother, those options would never get her approval. I could find my way to a place like Bonny, the base of expatriates working for the oil companies, and sell my body to a whitey. Some girls from my town did that in order to send money home to their families. They all had the same look, whether they sold themselves in Warri, Bonny, or in Port Harcourt. Their faces were painted the same—long lines drawn with black pencils over the follicles that once secured the eyebrows they had plucked out; a black outline over their lips, with hot pink lipstick painted within the lines. Then, using the same black pencil, they would ever so carefully put a dot, a fake birthmark, somewhere on their faces, usually high up on one cheek. Every girl had a different spot for her dot and, once chosen, it never changed.

They lived in the city, yet they always looked tired, stressed out, not unlike those of us in the village. Other people who left the village for the cities came back looking different, more relaxed and even more attractive than they had looked in the village. Some of these girls came back looking as though they had never left the village, making you wonder if somehow they missed the city breeze that we all dreamed could transform us into robust, good-looking people.

Their faces looked tight like they spent all day, as those of us in the village did, with their heads under a pot, blowing into the embers of firewood to keep the fire going. Some of them came back with skin that looked like someone had touched wet coal and rubbed it over them tauntingly—some here, some there. Their faces, hands, legs, and feet were yellow, though some parts had big smudges of black. Their skin had an acrid smell, worse than the odour of festering wounds, which they tried to bury under scented powders and perfumes. We were told that these were all the effects of the chemicals in the creams they used to bleach their skins.. The funny thing was that they admired themselves in mirrors and spoke with pride about the city beauty creams that made their skin look "smooth," as if they could not see and smell what the rest of us could. Perhaps they forgot that some of us could still remember that they had flawless, ebony-dark complexions before they left the village! Some of them would even compare their new complexions to mine, saying how they were almost as yellow as I was. I could not understand why anyone would want skin colour that sometimes betrayed one's innermost feelings, from embarrassment to excitement.

These women never came into town quietly. Whether they came by boat or by car, they planned their arrival carefully. It was timed so that even those who went out to farm would have returned and could be called on someday to bear witness to the flamboyance of the outfit that had carefully been selected for the journey and the size of the bags with which they arrived. These journeys were infrequent, so it was definitely a big deal.

Invariably, once the visitors arrived at the riverbank or at the corner of town where buses dropped off passengers, two or three people who were delighted to see them would recognise them. One of these people would then run ahead to announce to the village that the visitor had arrived; by the time the visitor reached the family house, a sizeable group would have gathered around to welcome them. Everyone in the visitor's family scurried to make them comfortable. Surely, for the service, a portion of the goodies from the city would be left in the family's possession at the end of the trip. The at-your-feet service lasted only a few days, at most a week, before the euphoria was gone and the demands of farming ordered the visitor's relatives away from the excitement; therefore, the shorter the trip, the better it was for the visitor.

Many young girls were eager to follow in the path of these visitors. They dreamed of a life that would allow them enough cash to buy nice clothes, send money home once a month, and make the occasional impressive visits to the village. When our visitors had the ears of those young girls eager to follow in their path and taste the life they were living, they would reveal the rules of the cutthroat game of survival they played wherever they were situated.

"My sister, show us de way now?" an eager voice would ask.

"So tell us, how una dey manage for dat side?" another would throw in.

With a look of disdain, our visitor would scan the faces of each of the eager village girls as if to read their souls and then, determining that they were all weak-hearted, bait their curiosity with, "You girls think you can survive that life?"

"Tell us, see how fresh you look; you just don't want us to enjoy with you," they would reply eagerly.

"It is not easy o!" came the warning.

Then the visitors would reveal what was available on the menu. The whiteys were always the catch of the day. Whiteys gave a lot of money; bought gifts; rented flats for their girls; and, if the girls were lucky and had the right native doctor, they could get their whiteys to fall in love with them and maybe take them away to whitey's home country. The Filipinos and the *chinkos* did not give as much money, but they bought many gifts, and they were definitely better than the *sykrawkraws* (the local men who, although they held low-level jobs in the oil companies, had little more cash to burn on a few drinks than the average local).

Girls did anything to get a whitey. If it meant travelling deep into the bushes of Isoko land to get a love potion, then it had to be so. If it meant putting a scar on another girl's face for daring to swoop in on the whitey they discovered and laid claims to first, then they were prepared for the battle. Whatever it took, they did.

Our visitors told of times when they fell into the hands of a crazy whitey who beat them up or pushed objects like bottles into their privates as part of the "fun." It seemed that, sometimes, there were so many unimaginable horrors to get through before the "clients" released the money. Nevertheless, if one were lucky, before they made the mistake of taking off with one of these crazy whiteys, someone else who had experienced his brutality would tactically stop them and warn them off him.

In addition to worrying about the other girls and crazy whiteys, they had to worry about the local boys. Occasionally, the local boys would remind the girls that they still had power in town. They would attack the shacks where the girls lived, beat them up, steal their money, and, if their minds had been taken over by the evil spirits in booze and hard drugs, they would destroy all the property that had gotten in the way of their mission. In areas where the local boys acted as pimps for the girls, there were cases where one brother killed another over the returns from a girl they were pimping.

After recounting all of these terrifying tales, our visitors would add, "And na our money o! Na our oil money!" By this time, some of the girls had their mouths open in amazement; some clutched their chests in fear; while others jumped up and down excited, as they pictured themselves in the same life, blurring out all the minuses in their little minds.

I had never been in a physical fight in my life. I could survive a war of words, but emerging victorious from fisticuffs was in great doubt. And if I went by my mother's words, the first day I had sex would be the last day of my life, so I knew that this had to be at the bottom of my list of options.

My other option was to find someone from our village who lived in the city and needed house help. I would help them with duties, such as cooking, cleaning, washing, going to the market, and taking care of children; in exchange, they would pay so I could learn a trade. However, there were two problems with this. The first problem was these arrangements never turned out exactly as agreed upon after you got to the city. Some children returned to the village with tales of how their mistresses would beat them daily, deny them food, and, after years of service, send them back to the village without having improved their lives, as promised. The second problem was my age. Most times when people sent for help, they wanted younger children, still in primary school, or much older women who had children who were no longer dependent on them. Yet another option was to learn a trade—sewing, catering, or hairstyling—and start my own business.

I was open to all sorts of things. The only option I was unwilling to consider, that tormented my quiet moments the most, was to remain in my village. My ears still rang from maternal wails piercing the foggy days when mothers mourned a child lost to sickness or to the deceptively calm waters that lay hungry below the stilt latrines, waiting to swallow the children whose unsteady feet betrayed them before they had learnt to swim. How many more times could I bear the pain like a hundred razor blades slashing my private part because the river water that washed it was the same water that received the waste rejected by my body in its attempt to cleanse itself? The water that flowed with streaks of blue, purple, and red, as drops of oil escaped from the pipelines that moved the wealth from beneath my land and into the pockets of the select few who ruled Nigeria was the same water I drank.

Farming and fishing, the occupations that had sustained my mother, her mother, and her mother's mother no longer provided gain. I had witnessed lands claimed by massive floods during the rainy season, the earth slowly melting into the rivers. Women rowed their canoes farther and farther away to find land for farming. In addition, every year it was harder to catch fish, as though the water spirits had tied the fishes' wombs, until people barely bothered to cast their nets.

My mother told me of the days of her youth when every husband was expected to give his new wife a dugout canoe that he had carved out and crafted himself. The wife would use this canoe to fish, earn a living, and help to feed the family. Those were the days when boys carved out decorative paddles that carried the legends of the Ijaws in every curve.

Those were the days when the Ijaw woman could ignore the nature of the Ijaw man because she had a means of earning a living and providing the needs of her children. Those were the days when Ijaw women cooked a fresh pot of soup every day because the rivers were teeming with fish. Their farms held plantain trees so fertile that there was more plantain than anyone knew what to do with—roasted, boiled, mashed, green, and yellow, the possibilities were endless. Those were the days.

Nowadays, the men were even more oppressive than the women alive could remember. They demanded a healthy meal when they were hungry, disregarding the fact that the women had to walk extra kilometres to get firewood or cultivate and harvest the food now fertilized by their sweat and blood. Cobwebs would fill the pots during the time that passed before the men contributed to the feeding expenses of the household.

The men claimed that, according to tradition, it was their exclusive right to make all the decisions inside and outside the home. Most times, because they did not succeed in the home, they drew the line at women participating in communal meetings on serious town issues. "If we allowed women free access to these meetings," they reasoned, "where would it end? The next thing they would want to do is mount their men in the bedroom!" No real man could accept that. It just wasn't done!

The tension and conflicts in the village borne out of frustration were familiar to me. Some women walked around deaf in one ear because they had dared to question their husband's wisdom in spending the last kobo in the house on booze. Women with distended bellies that resembled pregnancies, caused by uterine fibroids, were confined to their rooms because a diviner had investigated and confirmed them to be witches. Young boys threatened to rough up the Amananaowei and his elders because rumours, probably true, had reached their ears that the Amananaowei and his elders had received monetary compensation, meant for the village, from the oil company and shared it amongst themselves. These images darkened the canvas of my village life.

My mind tried to hold on to the images of laughter from my childhood: the moonlit nights that wrapped us as children, when we sang, clapped and danced through games, pretending to tell each other's fortunes, naming the species of food or dodging possession by a water spirit. The days I spent with my mother on her farm before oil finally swallowed it up. The day, when I was thirteen years old, that I took off with the girls in my age group to Wokiri, carrying soot we had collected from kerosene lanterns over several weeks, sewing needles, razor blades, and charcoal. We spent that day creating permanent designs on each other's bodies. We looked on with anticipation as we waited our turns and watched shaky, inexperienced hands try to reproduce the butterfly patterns identifying Kolokuma Ijaw women that we had seen on our mothers' stomachs, while the victim stood with her back against a tree and her hands stretched over her head. We laughed as some cowardly girls abandoned the ritual after the first cut into their skin.

My tattoo was not a traditional design. They had drawn an intricate pattern on my stomach, but I only made it through the completion of a circle around my navel. Besides the fact that I had very little courage and was in too much pain to finish the project, the girl who was pricking my skin to make the designs got scared as every part of my body gradually turned red. Some years later, I turned the circle into a flower.

I was afraid to leave the comfort of all that I had known for seventeen years to start life in a new place without my mother, who had been my protector, my shield, and who would have been, if she could breathe for me, my life support. Nevertheless, the desire to start a new life far outweighed any fears I had.

* * *

My pregnant friend Ebiere and I were sitting in front of my mother's house one evening after a party to celebrate with one of our age mates who had put to bed.

"Priye life sweet o, her mama throw party for her as she born," I said.

"Dat na life? She no get work, de pickin papa no get work, e neva even pay anytin for her head!" she countered.

"But at least her mama go help her wit de pickin. You tink say Bibi go throw party for me if I get belle?" We both knew the answer to that. My mother, who rarely allowed me to attend night parties for fear that I would "spoil" my future, would be the last person to throw a party celebrating the birth of my child before I had gotten her coveted university degree.

"Na party we dey talk? Man wey no fit pay dowry, how e wan care for pickin?" she asked.

I looked at her and wondered how she was going to take care of her child. Her mother had young children who she was bringing up single-handedly. Her father earned money that he spent every which way, except to take care of his family. Ebiere had no work. The father of her child had worked odd jobs, mostly as an electrician. Patrons had often called him to other villages to work on construction sites. He was not one of the troublemakers in the village and was in fact well liked by everyone; he was one of the few boys who women frequently called on to help with their harvests or with fixing things in their houses. Unfortunately, he was with the wrong crowd when he was caught up in a feud that took his life.

"How you go do wen dis pickin come?" I asked. I just could not imagine how I would cope in her situation. A few months before, we were both students, sitting in the same spot, worrying about school, exams, and how we would leave our village in search of a better future, whatever that was.

"I go care for de pickin now. How I go do again, dem dey troway pickin?" she asked, very matter-of-fact.

"No, of course not." I could not say more than that. "God has a plan for everybody," my mother often said, although for mine she insisted on being at the drawing table with Him. God obviously had a plan for Ebiere, and it seemed different from the one we had come up with. I quietly begged God to include an escape from the village in my plan.

My mother was in her kitchen cooking one day when I told her I was going to Port Harcourt. Initially she looked at me as though I had spoken in a language that she did not understand. Then, slowly, I saw anger creep into her eyes as she asked, "To do what?"

"I just want to go and try my luck and see if maybe I can find work somewhere." Clearly, I had no definite plans. I imagined that I could learn a skill like sewing through one of the skills-acquisition programmes organized by the government agency set up to address the development needs of the Niger Delta. None of the programmes had reached my village since the agency was formed, but I was sure that being in Port Harcourt would give me a better chance of getting my little piece of the national cake.

"Who do you have there? You want to go and become a prostitute in Port Harcourt?" my mother asked, every word dripping with as much venom as she could manage.

"Well, if prostitution will feed me, then I will prostitute, no problem," I said with indignation, and expected that the spoon in my mother's hand would land on my head as soon as I heard the words come out of my mouth.

"You are not serious; you want to spoil your life. Beautiful girl like you wants to go and throw away her life in Port Harcourt?" I could hear the fear beneath her angry tone. The fear that transported her back to her own experience eighteen years before; the same fear that made her ask, "Where will you stay?"

"I don't know. I can find one of my schoolmates to stay with." I shrugged, praying for a miracle because that was the only way my mother would agree to such a flimsy plan.

My mother sat down on a stool, head in her hands, weakened by the very idea of what I had just proposed. "You are not going anywhere, and that is final."

Eight days of silence between us; it took that long to get my mother to allow me to go to Port Harcourt. During that time, she went to speak with the pastor of her church about the matter and came home one day to inform me that Pastor Ikechukwu was going to help me find a place to stay in Port Harcourt. I was surprised. I had not expected my mother to change her mind, at least not so soon. It was as though she also had been thinking that my evolution into the life she dreamed of for me was halting and would soon stop completely if I remained in the village. My mother must have seen the determination in my eyes as I defiantly challenged her for the first time in my life.

I left my village before dawn one day without saying good-bye to anyone. My mother and Mama Ebiye had asked me to keep my departure a secret so that if anyone did not want me to progress successfully, they would not have time to plan evil against me. The night before my departure, Mama Ebiye came over with a small bottle of whisky that she said she had been saving for a special occasion. She opened the bottle and poured libation, calling on our ancestors to be with me in Port Harcourt.

"Yellow, when you reach Port Harcourt, do not disgrace us there o!" she said.

"I've told her. This is an opportunity many are looking for; if she spoils it, she is on her own," my mother added.

Mama Ebiye handed me the shot glass and poured some whisky into it. As I sipped, both women threw out words of advice: "When they ask you to do something, don't argue; just do it." "Be useful." "Don't be lazy." "Respect the people you are going to stay with." On and on, the words of advice kept coming, occasionally punctuated with, "But Yellow is a good girl. There will be no problems."

I freely poured more whisky into my glass until Mama Ebiye said, "*Ama*, no pour de bottom of de bottle o. Na you small pass, if you drink de bottom, we go fine you seven bottles." We finished the bottle, ate some *kekefia* that my mother had prepared, and Mama Ebiye prayed one final prayer before she said good night.

So it was that I left my village with a note from Pastor Ikechukwu, written to a woman who he referred to as his mother, Madam George, and directions on how to reach her shop in Diobu once I arrived. I also had some money and food from my mother and a prayer in my heart that I would not fail miserably in Port Harcourt and have to return to the village in shame, having achieved nothing. It was my second trip to Port Harcourt, but this time I could not sleep for fear of missing something important on the way. This time there was no one to push open a path for me through the sea of people at the Mile Four car park in Port Harcourt. This time I had only the thoughts in my mind for company, contemplating the destination of the other travellers on the bus and wondering how many were like me—starting anew, confronting the unknown.

I had spent so many months dreaming of that day and thinking of nothing else but my exit from the village. However, when the day finally came, the reality of being on my own sat heavily on my chest, and as the bus pulled into the car park in Port Harcourt that sunny morning in April, I knew my life had changed. I was seventeen years old, and even though I had no idea what kind of life lay ahead of me, the feeling that things were not going to be the same again made my ears red and my nose tingle as tears glazed my eyes.

Five

I found out, from a man selling snacks in the car park where the bus had dropped off its passengers, that the address Pastor Ikechukwu had given me was not too far away. The man said I could take a commercial motorcycle, popularly called *okada*, directly to the house. Alternatively, if I was afraid of riding okadas, I could take a bus, which would drop me off at a bus stop called Mile One; from there I could walk, quite a distance, to the address. Just outside the car park were more okadas than I had ever seen, with their riders, waiting for passengers. I decided to take an okada directly to the house, as it would put me in contact with fewer people. It was my first time on an okada, and the rider could tell from the way I clutched his waist and drew long breaths each time he cut in front of a car.

As we approached the house, I saw a group of people standing in front of it, beside a white Toyota pickup truck. The okada pulled up just behind the truck, but the people did not even turn to acknowledge us. There was a man who, I could tell from a distance, was trying desperately to explain his way out of trouble with a mixed-race woman who appeared to be in her late fifties or early sixties. She was dressed in an elaborately embroidered *adire boubou*. Intricately formed pieces of gold adorned her wrists, fingers, and neck. Her gold-rimmed glasses sat on the tip of her small nose, and her mouth was crumpled into a small ball. She was standing with her hands behind her back as she shifted her weight from one leg to the other. Any fool could see that she was just about ready to reach out and release a heavy blow over the poor man's head. I had an overwhelmingly strong feeling that the woman was Madam George but silently prayed that she was not; if she was, this sure was not a good time to be arriving. Standing with her were two young women, one of whom was dressed in a similar fashion. She, too, was wearing a boubou, although it was not as fanciful as the woman's whom I thought to be Madam George. She also had on less jewellery. The other woman, who was wearing an Ankara skirt suit, saw me and walked over to ask if she could help. After I told her that I came with a note from Pastor Ikechukwu to Madam George, she told me to wait because "Sisi" was busy with her mechanic. The skirt-suited woman left me and joined the group again, probably to be close enough to hear every word of the unfolding drama.

I stood nervously for what felt like a whole day before Madam George turned to the woman. "Clara, who is she looking for?"

"She is looking for you, Ma. She says she has a note from one Pastor Ikechukwu."

Madam George turned around, pushed her glasses up from the tip of her nose, and examined me from head to toe before she asked impatiently, "Yes, what can I do for you?"

I held out the note from Pastor Ikechukwu and curtsied in respect. She ignored my outstretched hand, and just glared at me. "Young lady, I asked what I can do for you. I didn't ask you to give me any notes. I am not in the mood to read notes right now. What do you want?"

As I struggled to form the words to say that I needed a place to stay and needed someone to help me settle into life in Port Harcourt, her patience ran out. In the same peppery tone, she said to the other young woman, "Lolo, please find out what this girl wants. I can't take any more aggravation this morning. Let me go and look for a taxi, because if I rely on this foolish mechanic, we will not go to Aba today." With that, she crossed the street, the man trailing sheepishly behind her.

Lolo took the note from my now-limp hand and asked me to follow her after reading it. It was then I noticed that a boutique occupied the ground floor of the building. Through the tinted sliding door, I could see fabrics and various types of accessories, including shoes, bags, coral beads, gold and silver jewellery, and carved walking sticks.

Looking at Lolo, I noticed that she was a little shorter than I was. Her natural beauty awed me. Her skin was the dark brown of palm kernel soap and was of the silky smoothness of refined palm oil. In fact, she had the glow of someone who had just been prepared for a special ceremony. She had small eyes that slanted towards her eyebrows. Her tiny long braids were tied up with a scarf that matched her boubou, keeping the braids away from her long neck.

With each calculated step, she glided towards the boutique and I tottered inelegantly behind her. The boutique had a big desk and chair in the back corner, and the room was furnished with two couches and matching chairs at either end. Placed in a measured manner around the room were cases and shelves where the merchandise was displayed while two large, framed photographs of a much younger Sisi hung on the back wall. She was stunning. Even in the picture, you could tell that she was a tall woman, and her plump figure was covered in the customary lace blouse and two-wrapper style of Ijaw women. Even back then, her jewellery was overwhelming. I could not believe that one person could own so many coral beads and so much ivory and gold to wear in one sitting. In both pictures, Sisi looked at the world with contentment. Her smile said to all it blessed, "Life is good."

Lolo gathered up some things around the boutique, simultaneously leaving instructions for Clara to take care of me until she and Sisi got back from Aba later in the day. She spoke with the authority that only Sisi's daughter would have, and if she had any indication from the note, she did not give Clara any explanations about me except to tell her that my name was Zilayefa and that I was "Sisi's visitor."

In all sincerity, I was nobody. Who was I? Nothing more than a poor girl from the village, hoping that a good wind had blown me in this direction to better my future. At this time, I was still on tenterhooks because Sisi could return and tell me to take my little bag and myself back to where I came from. If that happened, then laying my head on a brick by a roadside was my only chance of solace. I had left the village with no backup plan, but I was prepared to eat mud before I returned to the village with the same nothingness I had left with.

We soon heard Sisi's voice calling out to Lolo. In response, she picked up two handbags, handed Clara some money, "In case of anything," gave her some more instructions, wished us a good day, and then dashed out to meet Sisi. At that point, I liked her already. She had a low, husky voice, but there was a delicacy to it that matched her small, beautiful frame. In the corner of my mind, I saw a future image of me in the likeness of Lolo, and that pleased me. Thus, I jumped into her shadow, accepting the possibility that this figure, who had instantly intrigued me, would envelop my own personality.

Sisi and Lolo left, leaving me to fit into Clara's day. She asked me to put my miserable luggage in a corner of the room and to make myself comfortable on one of the couches. As I complied, she asked graciously, "You don chop? I get bread and tea o."

"I don't mind," I answered timidly.

As she went into the kitchen to make the tea, I tried to settle into a couch. I was tense, so every position seemed inappropriate, and I ended up sitting on the edge of the sofa, my knees together, my hands resting on my lap.

As we sat around consuming bread and tea, Clara wasted no time in extracting from me where I had come from and what my mission was. She teased me about being a JJC—Johnny Just Come—and looked very pleased to be in a position of knowledge above me.

"Port, no be like village o," she said with laughter. "You go learn boku and meet boku people, but you no fit survive city life if you slow o," she counselled.

Clara was from the same village as Sisi. She had come to Port Harcourt eight years earlier and lived with a friend until recently, when she had moved into one of the rooms in the building, which had four flats above the boutique.

Clara was very excited because she had company with whom she could relate informally for the day, and she shared freely with me, giving me as much detail as she knew on the lives of the two women who I had met that morning.

Clara pulled her ear in warning. "Sisi na nice woman, but when she vex, she be like fire o! E better you just comot for her way."

She looked at me quietly for a few minutes and said, "Like say Sisi young, people go say you be her pickin wey she hide for village, as two of una be *oyinbo*."

I laughed at the idea of being a hidden child, although being mistaken for Sisi's daughter wasn't such a bad thing. Clara told me that Sisi had one child, a daughter who lived in America, who she spent most of her money on, along with her grandchildren; the rest went to keeping herself comfortable. At least twice a year, she sent a suitcase full of the latest laces, wrappers, and jewellery to her daughter.

"If you see when Sisi dey pack things to send to her pickin ehn, you go jealous," Clara said, and clapped her hands for emphasis.

She stretched out her arms wide. "The boxes wey she dey send fit big pass so. Sisi no dey pack small box o. You, me, plus two other people fit enter one box wey she dey send to America.

"All the little trinkets wey she don buy throughout the year for her grandchildren, you go see dem dat day," she assured me.

"So how she dey send de boxes?" was my innocent question.

"Dat no be problem for Sisi. She always sabi person wey dey travel, and she go pay de person to take de box for her," she speculated, adding, "I sure say de money wey she dey give dem pass wetin dem need to carry de box and send."

Clara told me of how Sisi paid attention to looking good and being healthy. She exercised frequently, visited her beauty salon every two weeks, and treated herself to lunch in the Chinese restaurant at Royal Hotel almost every Sunday.

"You no see how she look? You go believe say she don pass seventy?"

I picked up my lower jaw, which had fallen from the shock of hearing Sisi's age. "Na lie! That's not possible. She looks so young!" I exclaimed.

"That is what I am telling you. If nobody tell you, you no fit sabi say Sisi old reach so. She be psychedelic old mama!" Clara squealed.

When she indulged in something extravagant, Sisi would lie to anyone who complimented her, telling them that her daughter had sent it from America or had sent her the money to pay for it. Clara said in a whisper that Sisi did that to keep "evil eyes" away from her. In Clara's view, Sisi enjoyed being exclusive, so it was also a way to keep people from buying the same things that she had.

Sisi had not attended school beyond primary six, preferring instead to work. She had been exposed to all the influences that had converged in Port Harcourt in those days, long before Nigeria's independence from the British. Sisi used that exposure and the influence of her elder brother to get contract jobs for construction and even food supply in the government-run hospitals. She opened her boutique soon after her first supply contract in the late sixties.

Sisi was so business savvy and creative that she was very good at coming up with ideas for projects that she would sell to the procurement officer of an establishment. For the oil companies, she supplied everything from toilet paper to pickup trucks for lease. That was how she made her money. When she started, she was the only woman in Port Harcourt who won contracts of large value from most companies, and she was the only woman, period, who had contracts from the oil companies.

With the money she made from her contracting days, she invested in real estate. She bought a lot of property in the area popularly known as *Town*, which was the centre of activity in the colonial days. As Port Harcourt grew and other areas were developed, activities dispersed to those areas. Everybody knew everyone else in Town, and everyone made an effort to be their neighbour's keeper. All Town children played together; all Town children ate together; and all Town mothers *kongosaed*, gossiped and backbit together. Town was where the crème de la crème of old Port Harcourt society lived. The nouveau riche lived in an area called New GRA (Government Residential Area), although most residents there were not government workers.

Sisi also owned property in Old GRA, where she lived. Old GRA was where the colonial administrators had lived until Nigeria's independence. They had preserved most of the houses in their original state—imposing, redbrick, two-storey structures, usually with only two or three huge bedrooms on the top floor and large entertainment rooms on the ground floor. Large grounds surrounded the buildings, and a little distance behind the main house, a small bungalow usually stood, with two or three rooms in a row, a bathroom, and toilet. This was the boys' quarters, where the maids and servants of the house lived. Close to the house's front gate stood a small porter's lodge for the security officers. Clara wondered why the whites needed so much space around them but at the same time envied the fact that they had it.

Although government owned most of the property in Old GRA, which were used for offices and as residences for government officials, many nongovernment people also owned property there. The nongovernment residents of that neighbourhood were people who, like

Sisi, were old money and had purchased their property from the indigenous government soon after the colonial masters left Nigeria.

Sisi did not do much for work anymore. She lived well off the rents from her properties, and her boutique was well known. She was an old-timer in the business, and she had dressed everyone on the who's-who list in Port Harcourt at some point. She was renowned for her impeccable taste in the most exquisite wrappers, laces, and jewellery, and had travelled all over the world to purchase merchandise at the height of the boutique's success. She had locked up most of her jewellery in different banks in Port Harcourt, although people still came to her to rent ornate pieces for weddings or other social engagements. Apparently, though I do not know with how much success, she tried to downplay her wealth as she got older to keep away the vultures waiting to take advantage of an old woman.

I found Sisi's life story interesting, but I wanted to hear about Lolo. I had felt an instant bond with her, even though we had spent only a few minutes together that morning. There was an air of confidence about her, and she had been very nice to me, a stranger, so I wanted to hear about her. It is fair to say that at that point, I was awestruck. Maybe it was because she looked young, close in age to me, I believed her poise, confidence, and youthful radiance were attainable.

"So that girl with Sisi today, who she be?" I asked Clara, who by this time had moved from behind her desk to one of the couches.

"Ah, she is Sisi's little friend o! Sisi no dey joke with her at all. You know dem all na de big people for Port Harcourt."

Sisi was a part of the old Port Harcourt's high society into which Lolo was born. Lolo was the granddaughter of one of the famous Leslie-Cole brothers. The Leslie-Coles were Saros who had settled in Port Harcourt from Sierra Leone in the early 1900s. Lolo's grandfather, Horatio Leslie-Cole, along with his first wife, a Saro woman, founded a high school for boys: St. Mark's Boys High. It was a top-standard school in those days, until the government took it over. Parents even sent boys from Lagos to attend. Many of these boys were children of Saros living in Lagos.

Horatio's first wife bore no children, and after she died, he married a Kalabari woman with whom he had five children; Lolo's father, Tamunotonye Telema Leslie-Cole, was the only son. TT, as Lolo's father was known, was a playboy in Port Harcourt and remained a bachelor for a long time, successfully breaking many hearts with his charm and good looks until he met Inema, Lolo's mother, on a visit to Buguma, his mother's hometown. Inema was barely twenty years old when she married TT, who was over fifteen years her senior.

TT worked briefly as a teacher after he got his university degree; then for several years he ran a club that showcased young musical talent. Many older people remembered the club as a groovy hangout and the place to be for the elite. In as much as his club kept him busy, he found time during these years to hold several political appointments, including chairing the Schools Management Board and heading the State Electoral Board during the Second Republic. As his clientele grew older and patronage declined, because of newer, more modern establishments, TT decided to shut down his club in 1990. Then with a new government in the state, TT found himself in the wrong clique, and that was the end of political appointments, leaving him idle for several years.

Finally, more out of inactivity and a feeling of impotence, TT accepted a post—which most people considered to be inferior—from the military administrator of the state, to head a social and cultural development committee. The committee was redundant, had no funds, and could not make any decisions. However, it existed; it paid service allowances to its members, and occasionally, the government allowed it to execute some projects that promoted culture. Essentially, it organized events at the Civic Centre that displayed traditional dance and dramas, acting out the myths and legends of the different ethnic groups in Rivers State.

Inema, in the meantime, was very enterprising. While TT had his political appointments, which were prestigious but did not fill the coffers, she ran several businesses to support the family. Her biggest business was a sewing shop that she still ran, and it was through this shop that she met Sisi. She had been Sisi's seamstress, and they had become close friends over the years.

Between the properties that TT's family had left him and the money that Inema was raking in with her businesses, Mr. and Mrs. Leslie-Cole kept their children reasonably comfortable. TJ, Tamunotonye Junior, was in Lagos with his wife and children; Nimi and Bobo were both living in America, but they came home to visit their parents often. They sent all the boys in the house to school in England after primary school, but Lolo, the baby and the only girl of the house, stayed home, close to Ma and Pa.

Lolo graduated with a degree in French from the University of Port Harcourt and started trading in her final year, which she spent mostly in Lomé, on her final year internship. During her breaks, she would bring home clothes and shoes that she had purchased in Lomé to sell to her classmates.

After Lolo graduated, she spent her year of National Youth Service Corps (or Now Your Suffering Continues) working with the oil company, Elf Acquitane in Lagos. Everyone had expected her to remain in Lagos once her year was up, to pursue a permanent job with Elf, but she returned to Port Harcourt instead. The move turned out to be to her parents' benefit, as TT was over seventy years old and beginning to slow down. Having Lolo at home made it possible for Inema to spend more time with him, away from her business.

Lolo quickly jumped into the role of custodian, managing her parents' investments and properties. In addition, she took over part-time supervision of the tailors in her mother's sewing shop, although Inema still looked over every garment and had to give her stamp of approval before anything left the premises.

I wanted to know exactly how old Lolo was.

"Lolo na small girl o. She is only twenty-five, but no take her age judge her o. She is small but mighty," Clara confided, her tone lower and less animated than it had been all afternoon. I wondered why Lolo's age was a big secret, or if it was.

Even though Lolo's parents and her brothers had been very protective of her when she was growing up, she was very adventurous. She knew the value of her name in Port Harcourt and knew how to use it to open doors. She used her connections to get contracts with the oil companies.

As soon as she started making her own money, she took trips out of the country, sometimes without notice. She would go off for a week or sometimes just for a weekend. She travelled for pleasure, but on every trip, she bought things to sell back home. If she went to India, she bought fabric for Sisi's boutique. Wherever she went, she returned with merchandise for sale—gold, clothing, accessories, etc. The fabric she bought for Sisi's boutique she sold on a consignment basis, but mostly she just sold to friends and friends of friends. If she came back with a lot, she would throw a party in her flat and invite the young, working girls from the banks and oil companies. They were the girls who had money. She also knew the wives and girlfriends of the rich men in Port Harcourt, so they were also on her list. She had different parties for the different groups of women she invited.

According to Clara, "Dat Lolo get sense well well. She go dey take your money but by de time she serve you wine and *oyinbo* biscuit, na you go dey tell her thank you."

Clara gisted with me all day between serving her customers and attending to a friend of Sisi's. She took a break only when she went to buy some meat pies and Cokes that we shared for lunch. When she was done dishing on Sisi and Lolo, she pulled the lobe of her ear as she warned me again, "De only ting I get for tell you be say, no make Sisi vex o. You no wan see her red eye!"

All I could manage in response was, "Na wa o!" The volume of information had overwhelmed me.

Clara seemed like a nice person, but I could not help but wonder how much of what she had told me was true. Several times as she intimated the details of Sisi and Lolo's lives, I was surprised at how much she disclosed and wondered if she discussed these intimate details just as freely with everyone who came into the shop when Sisi was not around. She had given me a lot of information, which I appreciated but did not know exactly what to do with. It was more than I needed, but I did not tell her to stop. On my part, I enjoyed her melodrama as she acquainted me with the two strangers who would become my family, my lifeline, in Port Harcourt. There was no hearsay with her—she narrated with the authority of one who was present at all events.

Sisi and Lolo returned to the boutique at about nine o'clock that night. They had returned from Aba and gone straight to Sisi's house. Lolo then went home to pick up her car and drive Sisi to the boutique.

Sisi was a completely different woman from the one I met that morning. She returned my greeting with a warm, "How are you, my dear?" I was encouraged.

Sisi sat down with Clara to look over some books while Lolo stood close to where I sat. She asked how the day had been and apologised for leaving me in the shop all day. She asked me to get my things so we could leave as soon as she finished taking care of her business with Clara.

Lolo drove us to Sisi's house but did not get out of the car, claiming she was tired and needed to go straight home. She told Sisi that she would return the next afternoon after she had run some errands for her mother and dropped off some papers for a payment she was expecting from Emerald Bank. The bank, she said, had been holding her money for too long, and she was tired of them tossing her around. With that, Lolo bade us farewell, and I followed Sisi inside.

Walking into Sisi's house, I was struck dumb. It was like nothing I had ever seen before. Sure, there were some big houses in my village, and Clara had mentioned it, but I did not expect to see so much free space around the house. I had thought that Clara was exaggerating when she told me about the houses in Old GRA, but when I saw Sisi's house with my own eyes, I felt sorry for the old man at the porter's lodge who had to walk the distance to the front door to announce visitors.

The front door opened into a small area leading up to some steps. To our left was the living room, and to our right was a very large dining room. We walked into the dining room, where Sisi asked me if I was hungry. Before I could answer, she pushed a bell on the wall and a woman who looked about the same age as Clara emerged from the kitchen.

"Esther, this is Zilayefa; she will be staying here for some time."

"Yes, ma."

"Make sure there are fresh sheets in that other room."

"Yes, ma."

"Well, show her where everything is upstairs. I will see you tomorrow."

"Sisi, won't you eat anything?"

"Just bring me some tea and some of the crackers I bought today," she instructed.

Esther asked me if I was going to eat anything. I declined. Even though I was a little hungry, it was late and I did not want to put Esther through much trouble. I did not want her memories of my first night with her leaving a bad taste in her mouth. I was a JJC and was very eager to please.

I went with Esther into the kitchen and sat on a tall stool at the edge of a table in one corner. I could see the boys' quarters a short distance away through a large window above the sink, just as Clara had described to me.

All the appliances in the kitchen were made of stainless steel. Everything was twice the size of anything I had ever seen. The refrigerator, the cooker, the sink, even the gas cylinders that stood outside and fed gas to the cooker through a pipe stood almost as tall as I did.

Esther put some water into an electric kettle and plugged it into the wall. I marvelled at the beauty of everything, at the ease with which Esther was able to do something like boil water for tea. Where I came from, it was not so simple. You need energy from your mouth and your arms if you were using firewood; if you were using a kerosene stove (usually old, rusty, and leaky), you needed special techniques to make the stove work. Either way, there was a great deal of mental and physical exertion involved. But here, Esther merely plugged in her kettle and moved around the kitchen, clearing away her pots, arranging this and that, and in less time than it would take me to get a fire going with good dry firewood, the kettle was whistling, spitting out steam and ready to pour out boiling water.

Esther put two teabags into a flask and filled it with hot water. She placed it on a tray with a cup and saucer. She then arranged some crackers on another small plate and was ready to take the tray up. The formality of the presentation on the tray, for a simple tea request, was a lot for me—I feared even putting my feet down on the tile floors in case I broke them. I imagined my hands trembling and everything on the tray falling to the ground and crashing to little tiny unsalvageable pieces.

Before Esther took the tea upstairs, she asked me again if I was going to eat anything; again, even though I was now famished, I declined and followed her instead. We went up with Sisi's tea and crackers, and as we reached the top of the stairs, Esther motioned towards a room at the end of the hallway and told me that was my bedroom. At the other end of the hallway was Sisi's bedroom. I watched Esther enter it before I approached my new room. I walked into a room the size of my mother's bedroom and living room put together. Even though I came from a mud house of high standard, the size of this room still took me by surprise. The generosity of space overwhelmed me so much that I just stood in one corner and stared at the opposite wall until Esther interrupted my thoughts to say good night.

I spent that first night in my new home tossing and turning, my mind chasing after the possibilities of my future like the wild chase after an agile chicken that senses its life is about to end in a pot of soup.

Six

During my first few days at Sisi's house, Sisi, Lolo, and I discussed my plans in Port Harcourt several times. Under the pressure and scrutiny of two women who I so desperately wanted to impress, when they asked what I wanted to study in the university, I offered that I had done well in English and loved reading and so would not mind studying English. Since I had not taken the appropriate exams, Lolo explained, I would have to wait until the next year. Sisi informed me that she knew the registrar, but expected me to put an effort into the exams. Lolo suggested that, if entry became a problem, there was always the option of the Adult Education Programme (AEP), which offered most of the courses that the regular programme offered and at the end of your course, you came out with the same degree.

I was not very excited about the AEP option because going through the AEP meant that I would miss the much-touted October Rush that was tailored towards regular entrants. I had heard of how all regular first-year students in the country were welcomed to campus in October, and this was the time for guys to "rush" the incoming girls. There were lots of activities and parties organized to facilitate October Rush. It was one part of university life that students remembered fondly, no matter how the rest of their time on campus was. It was also a time when bitter animosities were formed, depending on the selection pool. After all, some people went on to marry the partners they had met during October Rush.

Once it was settled that I would try to gain admission into university the following year, Sisi said I needed a small job so that I could earn a little money to take care of my needs. She offered to pay my exam fees, school fees, and anything related to my education. All extras, especially things related to being stylish and looking good, making *nyanga*, as we said, were up to me. Pastor Ikechukwu's note to Sisi must have convinced her that I was worth putting an effort into; at least that was one way I could explain her unreserved acceptance of me in her house. I was overwhelmed by her generosity, and when I remembered to pray, I thanked God and Pastor Ikechukwu for my luck.

Sisi met Pastor Ikechukwu while he was a seminary student in Port Harcourt. After his first year, he did not have enough money to return to his village for the holidays, and one of his teachers, an old schoolmate of Sisi's, introduced him to her. She gave him a room in her boys' quarters for the holidays. During his time there, he impressed her with his humility and she took an interest in his progress, taking care of his needs until he graduated. Because she held him in high esteem, a recommendation from him was second only to one from God. She said that, because of what she had read about me in Pastor Ikechukwu's note, she could see me becoming as independent as Lolo one day, if I was not carried away by city life.

Pointing at Lolo, she said to me, "You see this small girl? The reason I like her is that she is hardworking and has a lot of good sense. Not many young girls her age are able to fend for themselves these days. They are all waiting for men to take care of them." After sipping from her glass of energy drink, she continued, "We are all *workaday* girls here, so you, too, have to pull your weight and learn how to be independent so that you can take care of yourself and maybe even send some money to your mother. Then the next thing is to get your degree. When that time comes, passing your exams is totally up to you. If you do not pass, it will be your own shame. It is very important to have that paper in your hand.

My dear, let me tell you, though I don't have a degree and I am not waiting on anybody for my breakfast, lunch, or dinner, times are different now. If you don't have your degree, it will be hard for you. You must be up and doing." She clapped her hands to indicate the end of her little sermon; then she said to Lolo, "Over to you, Lolo. You young people understand each other."

As though Lolo had been eagerly awaiting the opportunity to mentor a young girl, Sisi's "over to you" was all it took for her to take me under her wing as a younger sister. We bonded immediately. I had never had a young person with whom I bonded in the same way. In the village, I had my friends and I had the elders who I respected, but besides my mother, there was no other person for whom I felt a strong attachment. With Lolo it was different. From the first day I saw her, because I so desired to walk in her shadow, I was willing to put my life into her hands, to be moulded by her. I sought from Lolo the same kind of approval that I sought from my mother.

I spent my first few days getting to know the people who would become my new family and the town that would become my new home. Esther was my guide those first days, and I had many questions. I had many things to learn, and none of the books I had read in the village had prepared me for them. On my first morning, something as simple as operating the shower was a challenge. I had never used a shower before. In the village, we took our baths at either the riverbank or scooped out water from a pail, using a small bowl.

Esther showed me how to get a taxi or okada, which was cheaper, from Sisi's house to the nearest bus stop. She explained to me the direction of the buses and where I had to change, depending on where I was going. The main places to listen out for were Aggrey Road, if I was going into Town, or Mile One, Mile Three, Garrison, and Aba Road if I was headed towards New GRA.

We went to the market, and I marvelled at how Esther charted our course from the house with ease. She knew how to redirect her journey when the bus conductor called out "Borokiri, Borokiri" and then actually stopped at Aggrey Road, rudely telling all the hapless passengers to step out because Aggrey was his last stop. Some demanded their money or otherwise made their displeasure known to the conductor and the driver. Others just moved away, the weight of the other problems on their shoulders too heavy to allow the whims of the two dupes to unsettle them.

The bus ride was filled with humour—the grumbling of the conductor and his threats to charge some passengers double the fare when he couldn't fit six people into the row of seats meant to sit four. The cries of women who claimed they had left loving husbands at home filled the bus as the driver made sharp turns. The conductor tongue-lashed passengers who dared to enter his bus when they knew he did not have change for large denominations. The ride was over when the conductor, hanging on the half-open door, tapped his hand on the top of the bus and shouted the name of our stop: "Market dey?" Market was our stop, so Esther responded with a quick, "E dey," because if her response came too late, we risked coming under full assault of the driver and conductor's curses for being too slow and inconveniencing them.

I had to learn quickly because, within two weeks of my arrival, Sisi and Lolo had found me a job as a receptionist at the Royal Hotel. After they had made all the arrangements for me, I simply had to go see Mr. Moses at the hotel one day. Esther accompanied me there, and we walked into the lobby, which was abuzz with activity. An organization was holding a meeting there that day, so the lobby was unusually busy. Some occupants had the luxury of having someone walk a respectable distance behind with their briefcase; others settled their bills at the reception desk, while one or two kept watch just in case their *ogas* needed them at some point.

It was about eleven o'clock in the morning, not the best time for us to be there, I later learnt. People were checking out and checking in, so the reception area was busy. Still, we managed to let someone behind the desk know that we were there to see Mr. Moses. They asked us to sit in the lobby and wait for him because he was busy with the accounts.

As we sat and waited, several men came and went. Attention from men was not a new thing to me. I was not the most attractive girl in my town, but when they counted village belles, I was definitely on the list. What pleased me was that, as far as I could tell, my village charm was holding up against the sophistication and experience of these city men. There were men of all shapes, colours, and sizes—from the tall, handsome species to the short ones whose bellies stood out as if about to bring to life a newborn.

We spent over one hour waiting for Mr. Moses. When he finally showed up—a smallish man with notably big eyes—he told us he did not have much time, so whatever we wanted needed to be fast. As soon as we told him that Sisi sent us, his demeanour changed. With a big smile, he said, "Ah, you are the one from our big auntie," and then it seemed he could spare an extra five minutes on top of what he previously had offered. He took us behind the reception desk and announced to the workers, "Dem don send us anoder mami-wata o."

Someone added, "Na'im good for us now."

I was used to being referred to as a mammy-water. I do not think anyone really believed that I was a follower of the water's mother spirit, but I had one of the qualifying characteristics—my complexion. Mammy-waters were said to be beautiful, light-skinned, and possessed of wily charm. It did not mean much to me, but in a place like the hotel reception desk, where they needed generous tips from guests to augment meagre salaries, it was good to have another mammy-water on board.

Mr. Moses took us into his office to have me sign some papers and to give me part of my uniform—a black jacket with the hotel logo embroidered on the left breast. The other part, a black skirt and white shirt, was my responsibility. Mr. Moses put me into the regular schedule; my first day of work would be the following week.

For my first week of work, I was put on the night shift because it was an easier time to train new staff. Lolo took my measurements and had the tailors at her mother's shop make my uniforms, and she dropped me off at work every day that first week. She knew most of the staff, and they were all happy when she was around because she never left without passing a few naira notes around. They all liked her and *oga*, Lolo's boyfriend, Kamal, who came into Port Harcourt at least twice a month and stayed at the hotel while he was in town. Kamal was a Fulani man Lolo had met while she was working for Elf in Lagos. That's how I started work at Royal Hotel with everyone referring to me as Lolo's "little sister," and that gave me enough goodwill to take me through at least a dozen hotel policy violations. Those first few weeks, I appreciated and felt lucky for everything that happened to me because I knew that not everyone who ventured into the city got good things thrown onto their lap, as I had.

I soon found that Mr. Moses was the most jovial of all the managers I had to work with. The managers usually had their hands full during the shift; however, Mr. Moses found time to joke around with everyone. He had four daughters, three at university and the last one in secondary school, and he claimed he could not wait until they were all out of his house. He complained that his house was the marketplace for information in the neighbourhood. His wife and daughters always had a congregation there. One of his daughters tutored primary school children in the evenings, while another one used the living room as her beauty salon. His biggest complaint was that he was practically being squeezed out of his own house.

Whenever he started his weak efforts at convincing us that his life would be more joyful when all his daughters were out of his house, we would remind him that without them, he would not be as pampered as he was. His wife would certainly not prepare snacks for him every day as his third daughter liked to do; she would tire of washing and pressing his shirts as his first daughter did; and even worse for him, she would tire of having only his old face to look at every day. Because he had his five "wives," he was looking younger and younger every day and did not stress us out at work because they kept him happy at home.

Then there was Monday, an Ogoni boy and a receptionist, who always had something complicated to say. He never used simple words. We all called him Prof because, in addition to using big words, he always tried to give us history and life lessons. My friend Emem and I were his darlings because we were both young and part white, which in his eyes made us special. His advice to us was to go overseas to study and, if we got the opportunity, settle down with white men and have beautiful whiter children. Being his darlings meant that he talked to us endlessly and tried to counsel us on what to do with our lives. Of course, this made everyone else happy because that meant he was not bothering them.

After the murder of Ken Saro-Wiwa, many Ogonis were smuggled out of Nigeria through Benin Republic and Togo to seek political asylum in Canada and the United States. So, occasionally, someone who had chewed on some pepper and had his or her ears full of Monday's wisdom would shout at him, "Monday, if you are that tired of life here, you are Ogoni, please find out how your people are getting to Togo so that you can join them and leave us in peace!"

Not one to take offence, Monday would respond calmly: "That is the problem with Nigeria today; nobody wants to take advice. I am just trying to help you."

The way he complained about Nigeria, everyone thought he should have found his way overseas a long time ago. Instead, he remained with us and made our lives miserable.

Emem was a Calabar girl who had grown up in Port Harcourt. Her mother, like me, was the product of a hit-and-run with a Portuguese trader. Emem was a little darker than I was, but she had light green eyes that gave her a supernatural look and earned her the nickname "Pussycat." We became fast friends because we were the closest in age and somehow just understood each other.

I found out there were generations of yellows in the Niger Delta area, and each one had a different story. There were the yellows from the 1800s, the days of the Royal Niger Company, later known as the United Africa Company (UAC), which the British had set up to maximise their gains from the palm oil trade.

There were also the yellows from Portuguese traders who remained in the region until the British took full control and pushed them out. In the communities that lined Nigeria's coast, these British and Portuguese interactions were the origins of the old-time yellows such as Sisi.

The next generations were those from the Syrian, Lebanese, and Greek businessmen and sailors, some of whom had married Nigerian women. These yellows knew their fathers; these fathers even sent them overseas for their education. They were the lucky ones. The rest of us were *born-troways*, rejected by our fathers or, worse, nonexistent to them. Our crop of yellows was full of variety, coloured by the Filipinos, the Chinese, the British, and the Americans who worked in the oil sector.

Folks in my hometown knew me as Yellow-Yellow, but I never thought much about the circumstances of my existence until I got to Port Harcourt. In Port Harcourt, being yellow defined my interactions with the people I met. Most people did not just ask where I was from; they asked where my father was from. I came to understand that people had preconceived notions about others of mixed race—they thought we were conceited, promiscuous, undisciplined, and confused. A mixed-race woman in a position of power must have gotten there because of her looks. She was not there because she was intelligent. There was even much less regard for *born-troways* such as me. We were products of women of easy virtue who did not have morals to pass on to their children.

Some people did not care, but even that bothered me. If they cared, I might have tried to defend the honour of the naïve Ijaw girl who had had visions of living happily ever after with a Greek sailor passing through but ended up with a *born-troway* to whom she devoted her life. If they cared, I might have even tried to explain that I didn't think myself better than anyone because I had the blood of a foreigner running through my veins and his genes confronting me every time I looked at myself. However, they did not care, so maybe when a man approached me, he was not thinking that I was of easy virtue because my mother must have been to end up with a *born-troway*. Maybe when Emem and I shared a private joke, people around us understood that we were just being normal, ticklish young girls and not brats with the conceited sensibilities of which they accused mixed-race people.

There were too many maybes, and my first few months in Port Harcourt I tried miserably to rationalise every maybe until I adopted Emem's attitude, at least superficially: It did not matter what people thought of me because of my complexion. I had to accept that I could not change the attitude of every person who saw my colour and judged me before they knew anything about me. It was not easy getting to that resolution. When Emem and I discussed the issue, I reminded her that she, at least, had the luxury of knowing both her parents.

I enjoyed my work at the reception desk. It was easy, and every day was an opportunity to learn something new from guests who came in from all over the world. Emem and I shared many laughs when we were on shift together. There was a lot to laugh at—people who got carried away with charges to their rooms and then tried to contest the bill at checkout time. There were indiscreet prostitutes who had been banned from the hotel trying to disguise their appearance and adopting new names to get into the bar. There were also guests returning from their business at the end of a hard day and pouring out their frustrations on us. Admittedly, the things we found amusing were not as amusing to our older colleagues, but Emem and I shared the same musings and were able to find the humour in almost every circumstance.

Not many of the staff liked to work the night shift because it was dead and therefore a bad time for catching stray notes from generous guests. The best time for that was during the morning shift, because as people checked out, they rewarded kindly the smiles that had greeted them, received their keys, and given them their messages. I ended up with many night shifts since, as the youngest and most recent hire, my comfort was considered the least important, especially when it came to scheduling the shifts.

The lack of financial gains in the night shift notwithstanding, it was by far the most interesting of all shifts. At night, the bar became the stage for the most peculiar dance drama, starring prostitutes and hotel guests. As hard as they claimed they tried, the gate staff were unable to keep out all prostitutes, although I had witnessed some of the regular "actresses" greasing the staff's palms with crisp notes.

Because of how rough things were in the country, you had to grease someone's palm to get anywhere, or, as in my case, you had to be extremely lucky. If you went to a business office for the first time and approached your mission with fear in your eyes, you had to grease a line of palms, from the porter to the front desk person, before you reached the secretary, who would also need some palm-greasing to loosen her lips about *oga's* availability and whereabouts.

Every evening, male guests would come down to the bar to ease the tensions of the day with alcohol. Many of them were expatriates, either working for the oil companies or doing business in the oil sector. Interested fellows knew their parts and played them well—a girl flirts, interested fellow buys her a drink or two, and they strike up a conversation if he speaks English (if not, they smile and gesticulate; language is never a barrier). The night ends in said interested fellow's room if he wants to take it that far. Otherwise, the drama ends on the dance floor, with whitey dancing like a headless chicken and his girl trying to understand what rhythm he is moving to.

The longer the fellow has been away from his family, the easier it is to woo him. For those who have recently arrived, the smell of their wives' perfume still registers high on their senses. By the time they have been away for three months, their senses can barely make out old wife in old country's perfume.

Royal Hotel was the only luxury hotel in the centre of the city, so it was always abuzz with activity. It was, for a few days at a time, home to civil servants attending meetings, to nongovernmental organizations staging conferences, to pilots for charter airlines on overnight layovers, and to businessmen coming in to grab the cash that was flowing out of the Oil City. Our guests were mostly rich men, and we had good regulars. Guests were hardly ever there as tourists. Port Harcourt was built for trade, not tourism. There were those who came in week after week, and still no one knew how they made their money. Our conclusion, in those cases, was that they were into drugs or shipping stolen cars. Whether their business was legitimate or not, they added to the array of moving fat wallets, the most important prop in the dance drama staged every night at the bar. Even the beadles who were there to be at *oga's* beck and call had a part to play, and they got in on the action sometimes.

I received my first salary, and although I had worked mostly the night shift that first month, I made more money from *dash*. I put some of my salary aside with the intention of sending it to my mother, but her letter arrived before I could do so.

My mother sent the letter through Pastor Ikechukwu who, in turn, sent it through the Anglican church diocese office to Sisi. She expressed her concern about not hearing from me and was disappointed that I had not thought to contact her as soon as I arrived. There followed a whole page chiding me on responsibility and good character; I was to remember my manners and be helpful at all times so that the good woman I was staying with would be happy to help me. If I had gotten so carried away as not to remember to write and tell her how I was doing, then she was afraid of what kind of girl I was turning into.

After her tirade, she went on to say that Mr. Diseye was happy for me and hoped that things would work out for me. His message to me was to continue reading as much as I could. My mother also told me that, naturally, my friends were all very surprised to discover that I had left without informing any of them. Some were angry but would have to get over it, she wrote, because my future came before any friends. She repeated the words that I had grown to hear in my dreams: "Your books should be your best friends. Spend more time with them than any other friends."

Finally, she mentioned that she was doing okay. She was still farming but looking for some other work, as farming was getting less and less profitable. The boarding housemistress for the secondary school had confided in my mother that she was planning to retire and move to Lagos to live with her daughter; she offered to put in a good word for her with the school authorities, if she was interested. My mother, in her usual practical way, wrote that she was happy about the prospect but that she was not going to put all her hopes in it. She did not give any details on what her alternatives were or what other things she was considering if it did not work out.

She signed off with, "With all my love, Ina Binaebi." I had always called my mother Bibi. That is how my infantile lips formed her name, Binaebi, and it stayed that way. When I got a little older and tried to address her as Ina in the same way other children addressed their mothers, she would get annoyed. I even asked her once what she wanted to be called, and all she said was, "I don't know; just don't call me Ina." As strange as it sounds, everyone had gotten so used to calling her Bibi that very few people called her Binaebi.

I missed her, and only then realized that I had not taken any picture of her with me. She had taken very few pictures of herself after I was born, so my favourites were those from the time she had spent in Port Harcourt before she met my father. She was young and slender then, with curves that betrayed the hands of a divine sculptor. Her long legs had the strength to trek several kilometres a day, yet they were delicate enough to make men steal glances when she was at the riverbank with her wrapper tied over her breasts and lifted over her knees as she bent to wash herself.

For the most part, after she had me, those legs remained sheltered under her wrapper as if under punishment. She always wrapped her thick, long hair out of sight with madras cloth. The tresses saw the light of day only when she undid the head-wrap to wash them. Her dark skin still glowed, although her hands and feet were rough from the many hours toiling on her farm.

I felt guilty; things were going so well for me that I had almost forgotten her face. I had been in Port Harcourt for almost two months when my mother's letter arrived; until then, I had not experienced the crushing loneliness I had felt the day I first arrived. My new life in Port Harcourt was progressing with more success than my fantasies had pictured. When I read my mother's letter, however, I remembered her voice; I pictured her sitting on a low kitchen stool, talking to me. I wanted to feel her skin, her hair, her lips; I wanted to be with her in her bed, with my head on her stomach.

Seven

When I was not at work or catching a few hours of sleep, I was content being Lolo's tail and experiencing many new things with her. Her maturity was inspiring, and I hoped that I could one day handle people much older than me with respect while getting what I wanted, just as she did. Being around her made me want to continue my education, and not just because I wanted to please my mother. I wanted to carry myself with the same confidence as Lolo.

Lolo and I had become very close. She liked me because, according to her, I was very smart and had a lot of potential. Nevertheless, she also noted that I was still naïve and needed protection from bad company who could lead me away from my education and from being, in her words, "serious about life." In a short time, she had entrusted me with her bank details and other things concerning her business. Because she did not divulge her business's details to any of her friends, I felt honoured.

Even though non-housekeeping staff were forbidden from entering guest rooms, Lolo would keep Kamal's room for an extra night after he left town and give me his keys. Then, the morning after he left, I would come off my shift, join her in the room, and we would order breakfast from room service. Sometimes she would be awake watching a movie on satellite television. I would dive into bed beside her, which is where we had our breakfast, until she was ready to get up. In the hotel, she always took her time getting up, as though she could not face the day without

Kamal. After she dragged herself out of bed and we started getting ready to check out, she would sometimes attack my eyebrows with the tweezers that she always kept in her handbag. Without fail, she also attacked the curls on my head with a handful of hair gel, to tame them, she said. I was her dress-up doll, but I did not mind because I worshipped her.

To her, I was the little sister she had always wanted, and for me, she was the sibling of which I always dreamt. I spent most of my free time with her and, in the process, learnt about modern living. I encountered new modern conveniences on a daily basis, beginning with the room key, which looked like an ordinary plastic card. Emem showed me a small gold etching on the card, which apparently contained all the information about the room so that the card could not be used for any other room and could not be used for the same room after the guest had checked out. Lolo's car door opened and locked at the press of a button on a small box attached to her keys. The only thing left was to start the car with yet another button. The way things were, I was expecting that I would meet someone whose car could be started and controlled simply by pushing a button—no gear, no steering wheel, just a button.

Lolo introduced me as her little sister to her friends, and I was pleased at how fast they all accepted me, though Lolo left no room for questions. She controlled most discussions and had a way of avoiding the questions she did not feel like answering. I thoroughly enjoyed the ride. I particularly enjoyed the perplexed look on her friends' faces, wondering where I had emerged from and what my true relationship to Lolo was. Moreover, for whatever reason, Lolo also thrived on guarding the mystery around her "little sister."

The only person who knew my story was Damiete, Bobo's childhood friend. Though Bobo now lived in America, he and Damiete had remained very close and Damiete visited the Leslie-Coles quite often. As he was well connected, he took care of Lolo's family whenever they needed it. If there was fuel scarcity, Damiete had a friend who could get fuel for everyone's car or diesel for the generators. If there was a shortage of anything in the market, Damiete knew where and how to get it. He was always available, and I think, secretly, Lolo's father, whom everyone called Pa, wanted him for his son-in-law, although he would never have been as intrusive as to say it to Lolo. Damiete was a Kalabari boy, so, for Pa, he was safe, close to home. Pa did not want to lose his only daughter to Kamal, a Fulani boy, who, he claimed, would take his daughter far away from him, turn her into a Muslim and make her one of his four wives. He always said half-jokingly to Lolo, "If that boy wants to marry you, he'd better start building a house in Port Harcourt so we know he is not capturing you to take you up North to join his harem."

Damiete was the all-service man, and he did it with all pleasure. Even I joined those demanding his service occasionally.

"Da, the next time you go to Abuja, can you buy me *kilishi*?"

"Da, Lolo is coming back from Lagos today. Can you please, with a cherry on top, pick her up from the airport?"

"Da, can you teach me how to drive?" Damiete had a pickup truck that he rarely drove. He liked to cruise around town on his motorcycle, but he promised he would teach me to drive his truck, since Lolo refused to risk us crashing her car into a pole.

Damiete told me that driving was very easy. "If you know how to use a sewing machine, you will be fine. You see how those tailors in Ma's shop use their hands, feet, and eyes all at the same time? You need the same kind of coordination for driving." Indeed, after two weeks of intense coaching with Damiete, I could move the car from first gear with ease, upshift or downshift gears effortlessly, and I could drive around GRA—all I needed, after that, was the courage to face real traffic on the highways and other parts of town.

Three thousand naira got me my licence without a driving test. The normal procedure required a driving test, but after adequate palm-greasing, the licensing officers did not insist on it; technically, anyone could get a driver's licence, even before they knew how to drive, if they gave money to the right officers. Damiete arranged it and paid for it, so it took only a day to get my driver's licence.

I displayed my licence with pride to everyone at work but could not get anyone to trust me with a car. On days when Sisi was feeling generous, she would allow me to drive her truck with her sitting beside me. But her constant fear of my inexperience, which caused her to tap my shoulder or touch her chest every time I went faster than a crawl, didn't do much for my confidence, so I stopped offering to drive her and she did not persist. I kept my licence for that emergency when someone would need me to drive or, better, the day when I would have enough money to buy my own car.

At that time in Port Harcourt, Damiete owned one of the three big motorcycles in town. The other two belonged to the Al-Malik brothers, Fadi and Khaled—Lebanese guys who were Damiete's business associates and friends. Their bikes were almost three times the size of the motorcycles that drivers used for okada transportation. They had bought them after a business deal that paid them a lot of money, and they were a novelty in Port Harcourt. Damiete and Fadi were very adventurous with their bikes—racing, spinning, and trying out new stunts—while Khaled was always more cautious, if one can be cautious on a motorcycle. In fact, Khaled hardly ever rode his bike and eventually sold it to a friend who took it to Kaduna. The dangers notwithstanding, I accepted many pillion rides from Damiete, despite Lolo's admonitions. I enjoyed the attention I received from my coworkers when he dropped me off at work. The exhilaration I experienced from holding on tight to Damiete, as the thick humid air hit my face, was much better than a slow and claustrophobic ride on the public bus any day.

Just as Lolo was my "big sister," Damiete was a "big brother" to both Lolo and me. He joked that if he didn't take care of Lolo and something happened to her, then he would have to offer his head as a sacrifice to his friend and her brother, Bobo, to make up for his carelessness.

When Lolo first mentioned that she would take me along with her on one of her trips to Lagos to visit Kamal, I was so excited I could not contain myself. I spent the night trying to imagine what the flight would be like and what the inside of an airplane looked like. I thought about places I had only read about, like the National Theatre that had hosted the 1977 Festival of Arts and Culture (FESTAC) in its heyday. The building looked so magnificent in books, and I wondered how it looked two decades after FESTAC '77, especially with news reports that the building was sinking. I wanted to go to Broad Street where, I had heard from people at work, touts could snatch your necklace off your neck so cleanly you would not feel a thing. I wanted to feel under my feet the sand of the angry Bar Beach, whose waters had swallowed many children, yet not enough to keep her calm. Some places I had read about and now would have the opportunity to see with my own eyes. I wanted to experience Lagos's go-slow traffic, the kind that Kamal always complained about, and the same kind that made him sometimes miss his scheduled flights to Port Harcourt.

As the day of the trip drew closer, I lost my adventurous spirit and dread set in. My thoughts were stuck on the plane that had crashed in the middle of nowhere almost a year before. I half-prayed that something would come up to make Lolo cancel the trip, but that did not happen. I began to pay close attention to time and realized that the forty-five-minute flight could feel like forty-five hours. I expressed my fears to Damiete, and he tried to assure me with the logic that I had nothing to worry about because sometimes the ground needed to be fed, and since it had recently been fed, it would not be looking for more people anytime soon. Of course, those words did not assuage my fear; if anything, the supernatural connection heightened my anxiety.

The night before my trip to Lagos with Lolo, Damiete was with us in Lolo's section of her parents' house. He had brought some things for Pa and had come by to confirm our flight time so that he could arrange to take us to the airport. That night, Damiete came with a pack of butter mints for me. He brought them because, as he explained, I would need to suck on them to unblock my ears, if the cabin pressure made them hurt. He gave the mints to me and teased, "Now you have an excuse to eat sweets, but when all your teeth fall out, even Dr. Pepple won't be able to save you."

He spent a little time with us, and before he left, he begged me, "Laye, don't go and disgrace us on the plane o! Just watch Lolo and follow what she does, although Lolo might decide to act like a village girl tomorrow." With that, Lolo chased him out and we spent the rest of the night packing and tidying up Lolo's place.

I made it through the forty-five-minute flight to Lagos with Lolo holding my hand and my head resting on her arm. She dozed off a little, and I envied her calm. By some physical power from within, I was able to overcome the urge to throw up. Just before the pilot announced that passengers should prepare for landing, my ears started to hurt, as Damiete had warned. I wanted to speak, but I could not hear the first word I spoke, so I threw a butter mint into my mouth and gave one to Lolo. All this I did with difficulty, with one hand, as I could not let go of Lolo's arm. I sat back and closed my eyes until I heard the wheels of the airplane noisily opening up and hitting the tarmac.

As soon as the plane touched down, there was a round of applause from the passengers. I burst out laughing, relieved that we had landed safely and realising that the hearts of many of the other passengers had been offering the same silent prayers. Lolo knew exactly why I laughed, and she whispered in my ear, "You see, you are not the only one who is afraid of flying. Don't worry, you will get used to it." That was my first experience on a plane; many more on that same route were to come.

We exited the arrival hall of the domestic airport in Ikeja and found Kamal's driver, Shehu, waiting for us. As we began to cross the Third Mainland Bridge, my eyes saw an unimaginable wonder. The bridge ran so long. The little flyovers we had in Port Harcourt, which had impressed me as I arrived from the village, were nothing in comparison. Beneath us was a lagoon and patches of swampland. Scattered on either side of the bridge were stilt houses, some in clusters that suggested a community. I sat dumbstruck in the car and took in the scenery as Lolo chatted with Shehu about Kamal's whereabouts.

Kamal was not at home when we got there. However, everyone, from the gatekeeper to the cook, knew Lolo as the madam of the house. We settled in and Lolo showed me around the four-bedroom duplex, which she had helped Kamal decorate. It was an old house that Kamal had bought and refurbished. Lolo had picked out everything from the furniture to the tiles in the bathroom. The living room was bare compared to Sisi's living room, but it was elegant. There were no family pictures on the wall, like at Sisi's. Instead, he had two paintings, one depicting a polo match and the other a veiled woman with sparkling eyes encircled with kohl. His television was so imposing; it took up almost one side of the room. It was the largest television set I had ever seen in my life.

Kamal telephoned to explain that he had been called to the office that morning and would be home later that afternoon. Needing to fill time before Kamal came home, Lolo and I took off to see Lagos. She took me to Mega Plaza, a large shopping centre, where, for the first time in my life, I tasted ice cream that was not vanilla. There were so many flavours to choose from, and I finally settled on butter pecan, which tasted like toffee sweets.

We left Mega Plaza and drove to Ikeja, to Allen Avenue, a long road lined with expensive boutiques and beauty shops. Our destination was Bella's, a jewellery shop that sold costume jewellery and made special-order jewellery. On her last visit to Lagos, Lolo had left Bella's some multicoloured precious stone beads that she had bought in Jos to string with gold links to make a matching necklace and bracelet. We were there to pick them up, but Madam Bella was not in the shop, and her sales staff had no idea where the pieces were.

We left Bella's and stopped at a few other boutiques owned by Lolo's friends. The time passed between window-shopping and *gisting* with her friends on everything from the latest fashion styles in the market to who was dating whom in the military government.

It was almost six o'clock when we got back to Ikoyi. Kamal had returned home but had gone out again. Jean, Kamal's Togolese cook, had started preparing some kind of casserole with rabbit. We sat in the kitchen with him as he methodically prepared the food. Every slice of tomato had to be equal. He cut every cube of potato evenly. All the ingredients were already prepared and placed on little saucers on a counter along one side of the kitchen. He did not open his pots every minute, as was my habit. His little frame moved about the kitchen as he made the dessert and salad, and he cleaned up as he went along.

Dinner was ready by the time Kamal returned. Jean served us a salad that I didn't quite enjoy. It was too raw—raw carrots, raw lettuce, and cucumbers. It was not the regular salad I was used to, which consisted of cooked carrots, boiled potatoes, hard-boiled eggs, maybe a few mashed sardines, and a good helping of Heinz's creamy salad dressing. Even the dressing for his salad, which Kamal and Lolo raved about, was a mixture of olive oil, balsamic vinegar, and spices. I wanted my salad cooked and drenched in Heinz salad dressing. I picked at the salad but enjoyed the rabbit casserole immensely because, although I had never had it prepared in a casserole, I liked rabbit and it was cooked! Dessert was something called crème brûlée. It tasted like custard, which I had been accustomed to because Sisi sometimes had custard and biscuits for breakfast. All of this was washed down with red wine, which my taste buds did not welcome.

Lolo and Kamal raved about the wine, its full body and so on, and all I could appreciate was that it tasted sour.

I told Lolo about the places that I dreamt about seeing so, later that night, Kamal drove us out to Bar Beach. Kamal explained that the beach's night character was very different from the day. During the day, families relaxed, rode horses, and enjoyed the sea breeze. Everyone was aware of how hungry the Atlantic was, and only the foolish ventured into her belly. There were stories of children sucked into her ravenous stomach as they played around the shore. Some were lucky and she spat them out, back into our world. The others remained in her belly, never to be seen again, joining the number of human sacrifices that sought, seemingly without success, to appease the Atlantic.

At night, the beach teemed with marijuana dealers and their patrons, prostitutes looking for customers and area boys looking for ways to hustle someone out of a few hundred naira. Luxury cars were spread around—Jeeps, Mercedes-Benzes, Range Rovers, and more. I had seen some of these cars in magazines but never imagined that they would be in Nigeria. There were luxury cars in Port Harcourt, but those parked at the beach that night totalled more than those in all of Port Harcourt.

The thatch structures scattered around the beach turned into makeshift bars at night. We patronised one of those bars, run by an Ijaw woman named Mama Rivers. We ordered one plate of pepper soup made with tilapia but only because I wanted to taste the famous Mama Rivers's pepper soup. Everyone else had beers; I was allowed only half a bottle of beer, diluted with Fanta orange, a mix they called *shandy*. Lolo said she did not want to encourage me to be bad and get spoilt under her watch.

The pepper soup was very good. Kamal had the largest part of the fish, and after he was done, the feast began for Lolo and me. We took apart the fish head and devoured every piece of cartilage, tissue, and bone. Kamal looked at us, thoroughly disgusted, and concluded that only children raised in coastal cities could stomach the mess of fish head. For Lolo and me, who grew up in cultures where the fish head was reserved for the father or the most senior person in the house, it was a delicacy.

The cool saltwater breeze from the ocean touched our faces, and the moon and stars called on us from above. All we needed, if we were going to spend the night at the beach, were mats to spread out on the sand, where we would lie until the morning sun chased away the hospitable night sky.

We noticed a man standing close to the shoreline, challenging the angry voice of the ocean. Where Lolo and I came from, people did not play around water so late at night. The rivers and the oceans were the resting places of sundry spirits, and when they came out at night, they did not like to be disturbed. All those who had seen them, and lived to tell the tale through our traditional dances, had done so from a distance. We believed that if you got too close, you would not return from the water. Therefore, at night we left the waters for the spirits and only ventured close, accompanied by soothsayers, when the spirits asked us to offer sacrifices.

Another man went around with his guitar, entertaining beachgoers, singing mostly classic reggae tunes and then spicing them up with a few of his own. He got around to our table, and we joined in, clapping in accompaniment and singing along when we knew the words. Our collective singing was not so bad, but the originals needed a lot more work. Kamal parted with two hundred naira for the man's effort. Pocketing the money, the entertainer moved on to the next table and continued his performance, the two hundred naira from Kamal gladdening his heart and making his voice sweeter for the next audience.

After the beach, we headed off to a nightclub so that I could experience Lagos nightlife, which, I was told, was very different from Port Harcourt's. Everything about Lagos was exaggerated compared to Port

Harcourt—houses were bigger, there were more shops, women wore more jewellery, and there was generally more bustle. I had never been to a nightclub anywhere, so my eyes were shining bright in anticipation of the experience. By the end of the night, however, I was very disappointed with my experience in the nightclub. I had expected to dance all night long. I had not expected that everyone would be content sitting down with such loud and infectious dance music playing. Lolo and Kamal were playing catch-up, stealing kisses and basically doing all the things that lovey-dovey couples do. They shared jokes in whispers so I could not even join in their laughter. When I complained that I wanted to share in their jokes, Lolo said they were senior jokes, not for baby ears. She teased that, when I was mature enough to enjoy the jokes, she would gladly let me in on them. I sat sulking, but Lolo was too wrapped up in her interaction with Kamal to notice that I was sulking; even that got me irritated.

Wishing I was tiring my feet on the dance floor, my mind went to the many nights in the village, either at a traditional wake keeping or during one of our festivals, when everyone danced till dawn. Married couples arrived at the venue and separated. New partners coupled for the night, had fun, and then returned to their spouses the next day, hoping that the night's fun would not produce a child nine months later. There were many excesses at those parties—drinking, explicit dancing, and generally vulgar behaviour. Still, that night, I longed for a drop of sweat to break out on my brow, even if I had to suffer some vulgarity for it. I longed for a man to appreciate my gyrating waist. Instead, I snoozed from the boredom until Kamal took me to the dance floor, for the briefest dance, before we left the club.

We spent Sunday relaxing at home, watching movies. On Monday, which was a public holiday, Kamal organized a trip to Takwa Bay with a few of his friends—Pierre and his wife, Suzette; Aliyu; Yahaya; and Yahaya's sister, Zainab.

It was a fifteen-minute speedboat ride from Ikoyi to Takwa Bay. Pierre and his wife had surfboards, hoping that there would be good waves. I looked at them and thought, "Only white people would have such foolish ideas as surfing in these angry waters," although I noticed that the waves at Takwa Bay did not beat at the shore with half the anger as the waves at Bar Beach. Unfortunately, according to Pierre, the waves were too weak, so they gave up on the surfing idea. Instead, we teamed up and played beach football. Zainab played for less than fifteen minutes before abandoning the match, complaining that we were all too aggressive and that she was at risk of having her legs broken. She spread out on a mat, bought some coconuts and paw-paw, and just took it easy.

The rest of us ran around playing this football game with no penalties, making up new rules as we went along. Suzette and I were on one team with Aliyu, while Lolo was on the other team with Kamal, Pierre, and Yahaya. We ended the game after Lolo's team claimed they had beaten us by about eight goals to two, although that claim was hotly disputed.

We all joined Zainab, who was now reading her novel, under the thatch shelter and took our places on the mat. We bought more coconuts, paw-paw, *suya*, and drinks, and played cards. Soon, however, Kamal and Lolo took off for a stroll and disappeared behind a formation of rocks. Pierre and his wife also abandoned the shelter to get some sun, or so they claimed. I watched the couples disappear behind rocks and wished that I, too, had someone I could stroll away with, hand in hand.

My mind went to the evening I spent with Sergio on Wokiri Island. Instead of the resentment and anger that I felt after he abandoned me, I longed for the warmth of his kiss. His embrace, his heartbeat, his fingers tracing over my arm, the butterflies in my stomach—I was reliving it all until Aliyu jolted me back to reality.

"Hey, Laye, can I join you in your sweet dream?" My dreamy smile disappeared quickly, and I opened my eyes and saw the naughtiest grin on Aliyu's face.

"Leave me alone!" I cried. I was so embarrassed. No one could know what I was thinking. Little, innocent Laye's dirty thoughts could not be exposed; otherwise, Lolo's already protective grip on me would tighten.

In sympathy, Zainab pleaded on my behalf: "Oh, Aliyu, you are such a troublemaker. Why don't you just leave the poor girl alone?"

Aliyu drew me into his chest and enveloped me with his arms. "Haba! She knows I am only joking. You know I am joking, right?"

By this time, even Yahaya was laughing, and I just nodded and pushed gently away from Aliyu. His touch threatened to fan into flames the embers that my thoughts of Sergio had ignited in my body, and I was afraid that I would turn crimson red if I stayed in his embrace. It was good to be the youngest person in the group. I always felt protected, but it also meant that many eyes were watching my every move. I could not misbehave if I wanted to, and at that point, I had no imaginations about finding my own fun. I was happy enough being Lolo's tail.

* * *

Kamal had an important meeting at work the day we were to leave, so he apologised for being unable to accompany us to the airport. However, before he left for work that morning, we all had breakfast together; he gave me pocket money and gave Lolo money for us to do more shopping before we left.

Damiete picked us up at the airport in Port Harcourt. I saw him as soon as we exited the arrival terminal with our baggage and wondered why he had a blank look on his face. I ran up to him very excited and greeted him, "Da, good evening."

"Excuse me, do I know you?" he asked with no hint of a joke in his eyes.

"Da, what's wrong?" I thought maybe I had offended him.

I turned to Lolo for help, but she had left us and was heading towards the car park. Damiete left me standing in my spot, in shock, as he also started walking to the car park. Still wondering what I could have done to offend him, I asked, "Da, are you angry with me?"

"Young lady, do I know you?" He was staring at me blankly. "You look like a girl I know who left Port Harcourt a few days ago, but that girl was not as rosy-cheeked as you are, so I am not sure who you are."

"Da!" I punched his arm, relieved that he was not seriously upset.

At this point, Lolo, who had been ignoring the two of us, said edgily, "Now that you two have had your fake reunion, can we get moving?"

I had enjoyed Lagos, but Port Harcourt had become home, and my Port Harcourt family provided me with the kind of security that I could not imagine possible in any other town.

Eight

I was living life as if there was nothing to worry about, but all around me there was palpable fear, fighting, and poverty. The same poverty and discontent in my village that I was running away from was present in Port Harcourt. The only difference was that in Port Harcourt, people did not cry out as they did in the village, or maybe they did and the other sounds of the city swallowed their cries. There was a lot to complain about, but not many people dared to do so publicly. Lolo and her friends were making enough money to be comfortable, and their comfort numbed them and inured them to the realities of the poverty and oppression around them. In a way, I was also removed from it all, sheltered by the comforts that living with Sisi provided.

In all honesty, however, there was nothing much they could have done. All those who dared complain about the land's leader mysteriously disappeared. We were even afraid to speak about such things in our homes. It seemed Big Brother was watching our every move, listening in on all our conversations and silently doling out punishments. One after the other, people who spoke out against the government were jailed, attacked, and killed by "armed robbers" or invited to meetings where they were served poisoned tea.

When I remembered to pray, I thanked God and Pastor Ikechukwu for the life I was living in Port Harcourt. I had more than enough to eat, even more than I had in my mother's house. In the village, there were times when things were so hard that all we could manage were boiled yams or plantains with palm oil. In Sisi's house there was variety. There were different kinds of food for breakfast, lunch, and dinner. Cereals, baked beans, sausages, and eggs were breakfast; whereas, in the village, what we saw was what we ate, and sometimes that meant *fufu* for breakfast.

When Sisi and I had breakfast together, we would read the newspapers and talk about the news, but she always ended our conversations abruptly with, "Abeg, let us talk about better things. These people in this country will not send me to my grave with hypertension." It was our time to share and for her to find out what I was up to. Whatever it was, as long as Lolo was involved or aware, Sisi was all right with it. I learnt this after several "Does Lolo know?" queries following information I gave her about my plans for the day or the week or even my future.

Sisi and I were in her living room one Saturday morning after breakfast, going through her photo albums, which contained pictures of her family, when I confided in her. "I don't know my father," I said, a fact she might have already known.

"Well, I knew my father, but I didn't know him as a father. He never lived in the same house with us, but he and my brother were close."

"How come?"

"My father worked for UAC and travelled a lot. My mother allowed him to take my brother along on some of his trips."

"And you?" I pressed on.

"Well, she didn't think it was good for a girl to be travelling around like that."

"Did he marry your mother?" I asked.

"Did they marry our women in those days?" she hissed. "I don't know. I think he did under native law and custom."

She looked at a picture of her parents standing side by side, with her and her brother in their arms, and laughed. "Our height definitely came from him." Her mother's head did not even reach her father's shoulder. "My brother had his looks. I can understand why my mother went for him; he was a handsome man."

Then she turned to a picture of herself, pregnant, standing beside a car with a young man. "I was just nineteen there. That's my daughter's father," Sisi offered.

"Is he still alive?"

"He died some years ago."

"Sorry," I said.

"Well, that's life. The good thing is he claimed his daughter and treated her well, even though he buckled under his father's pressure that he not marry me."

"Why? I mean, why did his father oppose your marriage?"

"Because my papa na *oyinbo*. His son had to marry someone whose lineage he knew. You young ones today don't have to pass through what some of us passed through." She paused before adding, "In my place, some *oyinbo* children were killed at birth because it was a shameful thing to have a half-caste in the family."

I listened to Sisi, slowly appreciating the fact that knowing my father would not release me from society's judgment. At that moment, the realization was comforting.

"Anyway, my dear, you don't know your father and you can't do anything about that. Focus on the things you have control over. Study, pass your exams, and get your education. If you do that, no one can take your future away from you because your father is not around. Do you understand?"

"Yes, ma," I agreed, even though I knew that my obsession over my father's whereabouts would not end, at least not that day.

"In any case, only mama sabi who her pickin papa be and because dey say, 'Married woman no dey born bastard'; not all people wey get papa sabi dem true papa," she said, and we both laughed. "My dear, papa story no begin wit you and e no go end wit you. Just look to your future."

It was the only time Sisi and I spoke directly to our similar circumstances, and I appreciated her willingness to share her experience with me. It was more than I had ever gotten from my mother.

Nine

Many people did not read newspapers, as the general feeling was that the newspapers were packed with lies because any journalist who had the gall to print antigovernment stories was carted away and locked up for their gumption. Therefore, the news mainly centred around which human rights activist had been arrested, what political figure had been assassinated or "killed by armed robbers," and the new international policies against Nigeria. However, as long as the world was still buying Nigeria's oil, our head of state did not care from which international union we were suspended for human rights abuses.

Lagos bus stop was the centre of news in the city. If you missed a paper a day or two before, you could go to Lagos bus stop and find the paper there. At Lagos bus stop, the newspaper vendors spread out their many newspapers and magazines on makeshift display stands; if they ran out of space on these stands, they'd use plastic sheets thrown on the dirt road.

Though the vendors allowed passersby to go through the daily papers without paying, I suspected they had a way of making money because they were there day in and day out, with the latest papers. I doubt they were there solely for the altruistic purpose of disseminating information to the masses. Some people bought the newspapers, but those who did not were far more numerous. They milled around the vendors to soak in as much information as possible and even debate and analyse some of the headlines. Most of them spoke as though they had doctorate degrees in politics, and all of them had a solution for Nigeria's problems. None of them gave the impression that they felt threatened by the imminent danger that hung over their heads, due to their loud criticisms of government. But maybe security operatives regarded them as harmless in the grand scheme of things, as they never disappeared but were always there to share their opinions with anyone passing by.

What was certain was that if you wanted to spread a rumour with the greatest speed and the widest coverage, you needed only to whisper the story to someone at Lagos bus stop. The rumour was guaranteed to take on a life of its own and reach all corners of Port Harcourt within hours, as Lagos bus stop was also the oldest central terminal for buses and taxis going to different parts of Port Harcourt.

There was fighting between neighbours, between friends, and between communities. Things were such that, with frustration weighing heavily on everyone, even those who prided themselves on being easygoing and having no enemies were dragged into miniwars. Everyone who could afford it had their own little army they could call on to fight their wars, which were over property, contracts, even girlfriends. And the young boys who made up these armies were so caught up in the anarchy that they lost all sense of decency and respect.

People did not call the police to settle disputes, and even on those rare occasions when they did and a matter was charged to court, there was so little confidence in the fairness of justice that very few waited for the court's decision. The judges were so corrupt that a simple case would be adjourned over and over again until the litigants and their lawyers got the message and paid some bribe to the judge. Whoever acted quicker received a judgment in their favour. Such was the way of the justice system.

I met one Romeo, an Okrika man, who was guarding a house close to Sisi's. The house had a small kiosk in front of it, and I went there quite often to buy little snacks—biscuits, sweets, and sometimes bread. Whenever I got there, I always greeted everyone around but never stopped long enough to carry on any conversations. One day, however, someone called out to me, and I stood for a while contemplating whether to answer his call or not. I had seen him before but had never really paid attention to him; I had not even noticed what he looked like. He was a very tall, heavily built man with one eye that could pass for good. But even that eye was a sick greenish colour that made it look as useless as the cloudy-grey bad eye. Now that I was looking at him, he scared me.

On considering the danger I could be in if I ignored him, I decided it best to be friendly, so I answered his call; to my intense relief, he said that he wanted only to know my name and to say hello. I told him my name, and when he asked where I lived, I pointed vaguely in the direction of Sisi's house. He pressed for the house number, but I told him that I was living with a very strict woman who would throw me out if he ever came looking for me. Fear made me extremely pleasant, and I left promising to look out for him any time I stopped to buy something.

Whenever I went to the kiosk and he was around, he engaged me in at least ten minutes of chatter, nothing that really concerned me. With time, he offered an unsolicited explanation for why he was guarding the owner of the house, Chief Wariboko. According to him, Chief Wariboko had received death threats from a former business associate, who was angry because Chief Wariboko had taken him to court claiming that he had swindled him. Though this was the story I got from Romeo, there were so many fraudulent business deals going around that it was hard to believe one party over the other about who the real swindler was, especially when they all seemed to be involved in fraudulent business. The story I had heard from Sisi and Lolo was a world apart from Romeo's version, but I never told him that. Most of our conversations did not require much input from me, so I just listened and asked very few questions.

Romeo had tall stories about how he had travelled around the world, sailing on ships with Greek sailors. To prove to me how many years he had been around Greeks, he told me what he claimed were some Greek words and translated them to English. Whether Romeo could touch the moon or not meant nothing to me, because he added no value to my life, but I had to feign great awe at his linguistic abilities because Romeo did not look or sound like the type of guy anybody wanted to mess around with. He could pick me up with one finger if he wanted to, and no one could convince me otherwise, so even if he spoke Ijaw and called it Greek, I was not going to argue with him.

He bragged that he was so heavily protected he would never be killed in battle. He showed me a little pouch he had on a chain that he wore around his neck; inside was what he claimed was his protection. With his charm, if the heat of battle was too much for him to handle, he needed only to find a wall and touch it with both his palms and he would disappear. Whatever magic stories he told me were easy to believe because of the way he looked. His eyes made him look so evil that even when he laughed with me, I was still very uncomfortable.

I wished I could ask Romeo about my father; he might have known him if he had sailed with Greeks as he claimed. However, the need to keep a safe distance from Romeo far outweighed my desire to know a man I knew simply as Plato Papadopoulos. My mother had never discussed him in detail. She skilfully avoided the subject when I brought it up, so I learnt to live without knowing, but with Romeo's stories, my craving for information about Plato resurfaced. My mother's total devotion to me had succeeded only in suppressing, not erasing, my desires to know about my other half.

Questions about Plato's personality and his whereabouts nagged me, and the only person I could trust to tell me about at least his personality had refused to open up to me. The idea of Plato and who he was, was my personal battle. One day I desperately needed to know about my father and the next day he and who he was did not matter because I had gotten as far as I had in life, and hoped to get even further, without him. Inside me was my personal turmoil over Plato and outside was the turmoil of a nation; somewhere in between was the contentment of life provided for me by Sisi and Lolo.

* * *

Communities were fighting over who legitimately owned what land after more local government areas were created, after local government boundaries were reviewed, and after local government headquarters were relocated. Due largely to the politics involved in the distribution of funds by the federal government and the oil companies in the Niger Delta, all parties believed, rightly or wrongly, that whoever owned the land controlled the local government and whatever funds it received.

The Ijaws and the Itsekiris were fighting each other, as were the Ifes and the Modakekes, the Kuteps and the Jukun-Chambas, and the Bassas and Ebiras. Thus there was fighting in the North and the South. Nigeria no longer appeared able to contain her two hundred and fifty ethnic groups. Everywhere, communities that had lived together in peace for hundreds of years were taking up arms against each other over land and even personal insults.

People were convinced that the land's unpredictable leader was deliberately fanning the embers of ethnic conflict to shift focus from himself and his bid to succeed himself in the promised upcoming elections. Not that he had much to worry about, for there were five political parties registered to run in the upcoming elections, and he was the candidate for all five parties. That was the democracy we had to look forward to. But when people were feeling heady, they would say, "This is not Ghana! We are not going to tolerate that military in civilian clothing that Rawlings called *democracy*!" There was not much they could do to stop the train of realization that was slowly moving towards the station.

Despite not having any official political opponents, the head of state's succession plan was in such high gear that, in an attempt to give this campaign an air of legitimacy, there were groups rallying in his favour. There were people organizing the youths and others organizing the market women, and there were rumours that televisions branded with his name would soon be in the market so that all Nigerians could afford a television set in their homes. Everyone would have a television set, but *garri* to eat was another matter.

In actuality, things were getting more and more expensive. As petrol prices went up, bus fares went up, the price of bread went up, and school fees went up, but salaries remained the same. While most people measured the value of money with the price of bread or garri, those who had money, such as Lolo and Sisi, talked about the exchange rate. "Ninety-six naira to one U.S. dollar? I remember the days when it was two U.S. dollars to one naira. They will kill us in this country!"

Long queues at petrol stations were a common sight. People stored jerry cans full of diesel and petrol in their homes. Some carried them in the trunks of their cars. It was by the grace of God that more houses did not burn down when people lit their candles and lanterns when dealing with power outages.

There were cases, mostly in Lagos, where, because of the madness of Lagos driving, a car would run into another loaded with petrol and the two cars would explode, roasting the occupants of both vehicles, just like in the movies. The street commentary on the petrol shortage was extensive. How could a country that exported crude oil have petrol shortages? How could a country that housed four refineries be exporting petrol when its residents were suffering without petrol? And on and on. What was the Minister of Petroleum doing? Despite being a man from the Niger Delta, there he was, sitting and feeding fat at the same table as the devils of government and oil companies and forgetting the starvation in his own home.

At work, everyone was especially cautious because one of our regulars had confided in Mr. Moses that someone he had never met before confronted him over a conversation he had had with his wife in their room. Mr. Moses, in turn, warned the guest to be more careful what he said and where he said it. Of course, this deepened our paranoia. Thereafter, no one gave straight answers to any question.

As much as we were afraid of our head of state, he seemed to be drowning in his paranoia, afraid of his own shadow. He made very few public appearances, and it was rumoured that he was gravely ill from a heart condition. We could not tell how sick he was because he always wore dark glasses. As far as I knew, there was nothing interesting about him; however, Kamal's friends who were close to the head of state's children said he was a very nice man who even shared jokes with them. In spite of the positive words about this man, and as carefree as most of us wanted to be, there were constant reminders that we were under some psychological siege. There were curfews in almost every city, but the police did not strictly enforce them. The police task force—Operation Sweep—that was to maintain law and order pretended to be in full effect, but law enforcement was so lax, the police so corrupt, that if you had enough money, you could pay your way out of any police trouble.

One evening, Damiete and I were driving in his truck after the seven o'clock curfew when we found ourselves in the net of a group of Operation Sweep officers.

Damiete started with charm. “OC, how now?”

“Your particulars, please!” came the officer’s very stern reply.

“Ah, OC, we dey fight?” Damiete continued, hoping his charm would let us off lightly.

“I say your particulars, please. You know you are not supposed to be on the road at this time.” The officer’s voice was still very stern, assuring us that he was ready to make our evening miserable if we did not cooperate with him.

Damiete pulled out his vehicle papers from the glove compartment and his driver’s licence from his wallet, which was on the seat between us, and handed them over to the officer. The officer flashed his torchlight in Damiete’s face, blinding him with the light, to confirm that it was the same face as the one on the driver’s licence. After a thorough review of all the papers, which were correct, and after thumbing the driver’s licence to determine that it was not fake, he had to come to the point.

“Bros, your brodas dey hungry here o!” he said through a smile. The same officer had lost his severe tone.

“De whole country dey hungry, my broda,” Damiete cut in abruptly. He was now a little angry because the officer was asking for money. Ordinarily he did not mind parting with some naira; after all, police officers’ salaries were miniscule and very irregular, so he could understand their begging; but he did not favour being harassed and strong-armed in the process.

“But bros na we dey protect una o. Na we dey keep you an’ dis ya fine baby safe.” His grin had gotten wider; it was now his turn to crank up the charm.

Despite his irritation, Damiete still parted with a few naira notes before we zoomed off.

If the officers wanted, they could have made our lives hell that night. They could have decided they were taking the protection of the people very seriously that day and found a reason to bundle us to the closest police station. The funny thing was that we would have been bundled in our own car with Damiete driving and one of the Operation Sweep officers sitting by his side, pointing a rifle at him in case he had any crazy ideas. Once at the police station, we would have had to spend the night, and Damiete, or anyone coming to bail us out, would have had to part with more money before they released us.

There were also many cases of so-called accidental discharges from police rifles. The good thing was that, occasionally, a police officer who was threatening to kill an innocent civilian would mishandle his own rifle and end up killing himself. It was not unusual to hear that a police officer harassing a bus driver and threatening to shoot him over the twenty-naira pass for checkpoints had primed his weapon and accidentally blown his own head off instead. In our private moments, we celebrated those deaths.

I was learning that, in Port Harcourt, human life was cheap—very cheap. On a trip to Aba with Sisi and Lolo, just as we got outside Port Harcourt, we came upon a group of people standing on one side of the road looking across at the other side, where a woman had just been knocked down by a car. The contents of her woven basket—oranges, vegetables, yams—were strewn all over the road; she must have been on her way home from the farm. I asked why everyone was standing at a distance instead of helping her. In the village when someone was in trouble, unless the person had been branded a witch, everyone rushed to their aid. Here, not one person was standing close to the woman or even trying to help her.

I thought about the family she left at home after promising to return later, the children waiting for her return, some old enough to understand death yet others too young to even understand life. I imagined a husband and a grandmother grieving but only allowed the briefest mourning period, as they had to occupy themselves with taking care of the children. What plans did she have for that evening or the next day? What promises had she left with family and friends, with merchants in the market? Were her children old enough to take over her farm? So many questions and no answers, but the answers did not really matter because the woman was surely going to die. If she had any chance of survival, each minute she lay on the hard, coal tar, choking on her own blood, reduced it.

In an attempt to alleviate my distress, Sisi explained to me that because of the way the police and the hospitals operated, whoever took that woman to the hospital would have to show a police report that cleared the person of any involvement in the woman's accident. Most hospitals required a huge deposit before even looking at the critically ill, not to mention touching them for assessment and treatment. After all of that, if the woman did not make it, her family might accuse the Good Samaritan of killing their sister, and there would be more trouble. "Our hearts are all hardened. You want to help but na, do me good, do me trouble, you fit enter," Sisi said.

It was days like that that made me sometimes long for the seeming simplicity of my village. We had conflicts in the village, but up until I left for Port Harcourt, an innocent person's life still had more value, at least to those of us who lived in the village, than it did in Port Harcourt.

Ten

It was October, and Lolo was organizing a sixtieth birthday party for one of her father's friends. He was a retired admiral of the Nigerian Navy, one of those forced into early retirement by the unpredictable regime. He was not very vocal about Niger Delta issues and received a lot of tongue-lashings and criticisms from fellow Ijaws. What I found out later, and what no one ever mentioned, was that Ijaws headed all his companies and investments and most of his employees were Ijaws. From what I gathered from discussions at work and at home, he was doing a lot more than some other Ijaw men in his capacity were doing.

Lolo and I met with him to get details for his party and she introduced me.

"Admiral, this is my friend Laye. She is like my little sister," she said as she put her arms around me and pulled me close to her. I wriggled out of her grasp: I did not like it when she did that in public. It made me feel like such a baby!

Ushering us into his parlour as he spoke, he said, "So this is the one your mother has been talking about." He further revealed, "She says you have adopted a young girl who is turning out just like you. Well, that's a good thing because you are a very smart girl."

"Laye, this is Retired Admiral Kenneth Alaowei Amalayefa. Admiral, Uncle Ken," Lolo said before she took a seat.

"*Okoido,* sir," I greeted him in Ijaw, and curtsied the traditional way.

"*Seri.* I like young girls who know where they are coming from. We need more young Ijaw girls like you and Lolo. Where have you been hiding?" He sounded so delighted, as though he had found the two people who were going to save the entire Ijaw race from extinction.

"Nowhere, sir. I . . . I have seen you before, sir," I confessed softly so as not to sound too forward.

He opened his eyes inquiringly. "Where?"

"You were attending a conference at Royal Hotel, sir. I work at Royal Hotel." Really, it was not the first time I had met him. I had seen him before, at the hotel, and he had even spoken to me. He had come to the reception desk to find out where the conference was taking place.

"Oh, okay, that's why I don't remember the face. I don't see beautiful faces when I am at work, or should I say I don't look," he said through a mischievous smile.

He motioned for me to sit down, and I took the seat beside Lolo. He picked up a file from the centre table and handed it to Lolo before he sat down across from us. I was sitting on the edge of the seat, obviously not situated as comfortably as Lolo, so he winked at me and smiled. But that did little to ease my tension.

"So you are going to be helping Lolo with my party? I trust you young ladies will organize something spectacular and surprise me."

He gave us his guest list and left everything else, including the design of the invitations, up to Lolo. He said he trusted in her abilities, given how she had organized her father's seventieth birthday bash.

I could not travel around with Lolo to shop and make arrangements for the party, but when I was not working the night shift, I spent a few nights with her as she sketched layouts, took notes, tied bows, created shopping lists, and detailed seating arrangements for the party. I found out there was much more involved in planning a party than I imagined. There were so many decisions: how people would sit, what to serve the guests, what to serve it in, when to serve it, what music to play, which police officers to inform and pay, and even which youth organizations to court to ensure there were no disruptions during the party.

For Admiral's party, the list was an interesting mix of people. On his list were members of the armed forces, as well as community-based groups. There was a mix of society's high and low, and it was Lolo's job to organize everyone so they felt special and included at the end of the day.

They bought cows and rams a week earlier while Lolo hired women from Lagos to cook for the party. They had prepared everything from *jollof* rice to pounded yam and *egusi* soup, plus salads and, of course, pepper soup. Lolo was determined that people must not wish for any kind of food and not have it.

Admiral's two children arrived in Nigeria the Tuesday before the party. He was married to an Equatorial Guinean named Pilar, who bore him a daughter, Alaere, and a son, Seiyefa. His son was about twenty-four years old and his daughter about seventeen. They both lived with their mother in Spain, but even though Admiral and his wife had officially divorced when Alaere was five years old, he had remained very close to his children. He and his wife had been able to maintain a civil arrangement, which ensured that the children either came to Nigeria to visit him or he went to Spain to visit them, or they spent holidays with him in his house in London. Alaere was her daddy's baby, which was evident as soon as they arrived. She got all of Admiral's attention; he took her everywhere he went, though he complained that the older she grew, the more anxious he became because she was even more beautiful than her mother.

Pilar had caught his eye when he was on posting to Malabo. She was beautiful and smart. She had the Midas touch—any business she went into was a success, and it seemed as though she had done everything, including being the sole distributor for Nestle products in her district in Malabo. Admiral said he was drawn to her because, though she was independent and feisty, they got along very well, and their quarrels did not last very long. He could always break the ice with some mundane topic, and they would be friends again.

He loved Pilar; she understood him and tolerated his excesses. After Alaere was born, Admiral was posted back to Nigeria and she came with him. It was in Nigeria that their problems began. Admiral settled into life as usual with his old friends, in his old hangouts, and was insensitive to the fact that Pilar was having a hard time adjusting to a new society, with no independent source of income, no friends or family, and a limited command of English. She spoke Pidgin English more like the Krio of Sierra Leone, so she could have managed, but still it was not easy. She could have adjusted if she wanted to, but she felt that Admiral was no longer the man she had married. Therefore, when Alaere was three years old, Pilar left Nigeria with her children and settled in Spain. She had not remarried and neither had he, but he did have, in his wake, a string of girlfriends, often very young women.

It was hardly a surprise that he had been linked with so many women. Admiral was a very handsome old man, tall with no potbelly and a charming smile that made his eyes shine. He had permanent dimples and, when he smiled, they dug holes in his face. Whenever I saw him, he was dressed in traditional attire and had a little bounce when he walked. In my eyes, he looked so dignified. If I had the luxury of creating a dream father, he would definitely have come out looking like Admiral.

Seiyefa was a younger version of his father and was just as handsome. My first impression was that he was quiet and withdrawn, but I discovered later that he was very witty. When he seemed not to be paying attention to a conversation, he would add a comment that would have everyone rolling with laughter.

Cooking and decorating started the evening before the party and continued until the wee hours of the next day. Although Seiyefa, Alaere, and I offered to help set up, Lolo said she had everything under control and was highly irritable, so we stayed out of her way until she called for help with filling and arranging the gift bags.

By the morning of the party, Lolo had transformed Admiral's compound. Half-circle huts were created around a makeshift village square with canoes and paddles leaning against some huts. A band played in a section near the house, and other than the welcome address by Mrs. West (one of Admiral's closest friends), there were no other speeches until the gift presentation session.

That day was unforgettable. From the onset, it was spectacular. Mrs. West's gift needed no speech to go with it. She entered sitting on the roof of her gift as the driver steered it into the makeshift village square. It was a Toyota Land Cruiser with the vanity license plate reading NVY BOY. That gift was the highlight of the evening. Those who sought business and political favours from Admiral also brought gifts of expensive liquor, fancy foods, and electronic gadgets. Admiral would end up regifting most of these gifts to all the relatives and friends who hung around him, and I am sure those who gave him the gifts knew that he did not lack anything.

After the gift presentation, it was time to dance, dance, dance. Admiral did not want his party turned into a political rally, and Lolo's planning, which kept speeches to the barest minimum, ensured that. Admiral went around all the huts and spent time with the guests in every one. Some of the guests were people from his village who had come to honour him; others were his business partners.

By six-thirty in the evening, most of the guests had left. Sisi left early and offered to take me home, but I decided to stay and help Lolo. Lolo's parents stayed until about seven-thirty before Pa said his old bones had to go and rest for the day. Those who remained, including Mrs. West, were entertained inside Admiral's living room. They talked a little about politics—strategies for countering the head of state's plan to succeed himself, plans for addressing youth restiveness in the Niger Delta, tactical ways of dealing with the press, and, most importantly, lucrative businesses to create wealth for Ijaw youths. The discussions went on into the night as Lolo and I supervised the cleaning of the compound and paid the musicians and all the other services we had used.

We spent the night at Admiral's house. Lolo, Seiyefa, Alaere, and I found couches in another sitting room upstairs and shared our observations from the party until we all fell asleep. We slept in the sitting room until about four the next morning, when Admiral woke us up and put us in bedrooms to get more comfortable. Later, by the time we all woke up and dragged ourselves out of bed, Admiral had left the house.

After a breakfast of plantains and eggs, which we ate in the same sitting room we had slept in, we left Seiyefa and Alaere so we could go home and take our baths. I had to work later that day, so I said good-bye to Admiral's children and wished them a safe trip back to Spain. They had come only for their father's birthday party and were returning, via Lagos, the next day. I was going to miss them; over the short period, we had spent quite a lot of time together and gotten to know each other.

* * *

The pictures of Admiral's party that came out in the papers and soft-sell magazines showed beautiful, happy faces of people enjoying incredible opulence against the hardship suffered by the majority of the country. I felt guilty, especially when my friend Emem sulkily commented, "So you were enjoying like this and didn't even invite me." Fortunately, she did not hold it against me for long, but I could only imagine what my other coworkers were thinking—I was part of the crowd that was greedily wolfing down pieces of the national cake. Even if I tried to argue that Admiral made his money from his businesses, they would rebut with the fact that he was once a high-ranking government official and must have taken his share during his tenure to start his businesses. There was no point even trying to argue that I was not really a part of that life, that I was only a temporary guest to that life of plenty. I knew I could never win such a debate, so I prayed fervently that one would not start.

Eleven

I did not see Admiral again until almost three weeks after his birthday party. He came to the hotel for a business meeting. When he walked into the lobby and made his way towards the reception desk, I smiled. "*Okoido*, sir."

"*Seri*. How are you?"

"Fine, sir," I replied with my head down.

He was standing directly in front of me and had his forearms on the desk so that his body was bent towards me, and then he whispered, "You just disappeared. I haven't seen you since my birthday."

"Sorry, sir," was all I could manage to say as I raised my head to find his face only a few inches from mine.

I was puzzled, for I could not figure out how he expected to see me when I did not have an invitation to see him after his birthday. The only way we could have met was if Lolo visited him and took me along or if he came to the hotel for whatever reason. Neither of which had happened, so I did not understand how we were to have met. The thought of arriving unannounced at his house had never crossed my mind.

As if reading my mind, he offered, "No problem. We will fix that. I am here for a meeting. I will see you later." He straightened up, waved a good-bye to everyone at the reception, and walked away.

Emem was on duty that day, and as soon as Admiral left for his meeting, she gave me a look, eyebrows raised, expecting an explanation.

I explained that Admiral was just being friendly with a young Ijaw girl who had helped organize a party for him, but she did not buy it, convinced from the little exchange that she had witnessed that he was interested in me—and not just as a fellow Ijaw.

"The man wants you. That smile on his face was not for nothing. All these dirty old men," she said, rolling her eyes in feigned disgust.

"Ah, Emem, you need help o. You always think of bad things. Everyone knows the man is always smiling." I looked around and realized that everyone else at the desk had noticed my intimate exchange with Admiral.

"Not like that!" Emem pushed my shoulder lightly. "You better open your eyes. The man is loaded; he can make you very comfortable."

"Did I tell you I was uncomfortable? Anyway, stop jumping to conclusions. The man is just being nice." I was indignant and in a hurry to close the subject, because I could feel the blood rushing to my ears.

"Well, we'll see," she said as she snatched up a piece of paper lying in front of me.

I really did not give much credit to Emem's thinking but did acknowledge that she was more experienced in these matters than I was. In the brief period I had known her, she had told me of the several boyfriends she had worked her way through. Some she dated just because they gave her money. Others were merely for physical pleasure. Then there were one or two who she would have considered for marriage, if only they had proposed.

Emem never seemed to lack for anything. Between her work and the string of men who wanted to date her, she could afford most of what she wanted. Even though both of her parents worked and did not really need her support, she took care of her family and even made up tear-inducing stories in their name to get money from her male admirers. Her father owned a photography studio, and business was doing well, though it was a small business. Her mother sold cosmetics at the market. Between both of them, there was enough to make ends meet, so what Emem sent home provided extra comforts for them and her siblings.

My life was comfortable, compared to the life I had left behind. I was living in the lap of luxury, as there was very little that I needed that I did not have. Most of my salary remained in my bank account, since I did not have to spend much for anything. If I went out with Lolo, she took care of all the bills. I spent very little on clothes and shoes because each time Lolo travelled, I got new additions to my wardrobe. After contributing to my growing nest egg in the bank, most of the extras I got from work went to my mother in the village.

Since I arrived in Port Harcourt, I had been too busy to think of having a boyfriend. I shared my twenty-four hours between work, Lolo, Sisi, and, occasionally, my books. This may have been why I did not take Emem's warnings too seriously. I could not imagine where I would find the time to carry on a relationship with anyone, much less a secret relationship.

That evening, as I sat in the kitchen with Esther, the security guard came to the kitchen window to tell me that someone was waiting for me outside the gate. I was afraid that, despite my best efforts, big Romeo had managed to track me down. I dragged my feet towards the gate, rehearsing with every step what I would say to Romeo and how I would tell him politely that he was not welcome at the house.

I reached the gate, and the guard pointed to a black Mercedes-Benz parked a few meters away. Mystified, I walked towards the car, trying to see through its dark-tinted windows, as I had no idea whose car it was. As soon as I got close to the front window, I began to feel I had made a mistake by coming out in the first place, but it was too late; I was too curious to turn back. The front passenger window whispered down, and it was Admiral! My galloping heartbeat returned to normal when I saw his face, but almost immediately it started racing again. I was happy that the person in the car was someone I knew, but then I thought of my discussion with Emem earlier that day and wondered if I could handle what she had told me Admiral had in mind.

"Come in."

I opened the door and gingerly settled into the cold leather seat beside him. He was listening to highlife music. I thought the words, "Good evening, sir. What are you doing here?" but I did not hear them come out of my immobile mouth. I sat in the car, looking straight ahead into the darkness. I was too shy to look at him. I did not know what I was expected to say or do. I was shocked numb.

"You don't look happy to see me. Were you sleeping?" he asked, sounding concerned.

"No . . . no, sir. I . . . I . . . I am . . . ," I stuttered. I did not know what to say to him.

"I had to see you again today, because after I saw you this morning, I had a very good day," he said excitedly.

"Thank you, sir," I said nervously.

I felt something on my arm, and as I flinched, I turned to see it was Admiral's hand.

"Relax. I am not going to bite you. You do look like you'd be sweet to bite, but I'll save that for another day," he said through a wide grin. It was supposed to be a joke, but I could not laugh. I was too overwhelmed by the situation to appreciate it as a joke. Then he added, "So tell me about yourself."

"What do you want to know?" I sat, still nervous and feeling the tension in my shoulders. Even with the air conditioner blowing directly in my face, my palms were sweating and I rubbed them together in my lap. Admiral took both my hands in his, rubbing them gently, and said, "Anything. Just talk to me, my dear."

"I don't know what to say." I gave him a quick look and put my head down again.

With one hand, he turned my head to face him. "Don't tell me you are shy now. When you were with Lolo, you were jumping all over the place. Now you don't want to share your liveliness with me."

"I am sorry, sir." I started taking in deep breaths, hoping to get more relaxed.

"I left a meeting in my house to come looking for you."

"I am sorry, sir." I was still tense.

He pulled back a little. "Stop saying that and stop calling me sir. Do you realize how many times you have said that since we started this conversation? You have nothing to be sorry about."

He put his hand on my shoulder reassuringly and let his fingers roam, massaging me softly until he was playing with the little hairs at my nape. "So, you don't want to talk to me?"

"No, sir. I just don't know what to say." I could not stop saying *sir*. He was an elder!

He cupped my face in his hands. Looking deep into my eyes, he said, "Well, you can start by telling me where you've been hiding this beautiful face." I laughed, and he added delightedly, "Ah, she laughs. Maybe I will be lucky and the lively Laye will make an appearance before I leave tonight." I laughed again. Then we sat quietly for what seemed like a month and a day, with Admiral looking at me and me looking down at my lap. I felt as if his eyes were about to burn a hole in the top of my head, and still I could not look at him for any length of time. Finally, he said, "Okay, dear, I have to go back to this meeting, but I will come and see you again. Sleep well."

"Thank you, sir," I said. I was blushing red!

That was it. As I entered the house, I ran into Esther. When she asked who I was with outside, I said it was Emem. She asked why Emem had not come inside, as she did sometimes, and I lied and said she had come with a boyfriend and they were just passing through.

I could not sleep that night, wondering what kind of relationship Admiral wanted—mentor, quick affair or long-term relationship. He was not someone I had met in passing, and I knew that would make things even more complicated. I knew that I would need help in handling an affair if one developed, and I certainly couldn't go to Lolo for that kind of help. She would twist my neck before she endorsed a relationship with Admiral. I would not expect anything less from her. As crazy as she could be sometimes, after she had wrung my neck, she probably would pay him a visit and command him to keep his filthy hands to himself. Honestly, I was not sure what her reaction would be, but since she had been so protective of me, watching me like a hawk and telling men who expressed interest in me that I was too young for them, I knew she would not approve. I also was not prepared to find out, for I saw no use in rocking my steady boat.

Lying in bed, my brain struggling to process a million thoughts, I realized that, in my case, seventeen years is not enough time to learn the things one needs to know in order to have any kind of relationship with a sixty-year-old man. When I met Sergio, I was desperate and that undoubtedly affected the clarity of my thought processes. I had looked at my options and settled on absconding with a man, not minding his age. Now, faced with the hot pursuit of an older man, I was not quite sure how to handle myself. Yes, I was charming, and I knew how to flirt, but I had never had the courage to go beyond flirting. I had a feeling there was nowhere to run or hide from Admiral, and I was not sure I wanted to. I was curious about this experience, the comfort that Emem had hinted at.

At work the next day, I told Emem about Admiral's visit. "I told you," she squealed excitedly. "If you like be acting like a baby."

"Emem, I am in trouble. What am I going to do?" I asked, revealing my apprehension.

"Just relax, my dear. You are lucky; you will have someone who knows what he is doing for your first time." She scrunched up her face and revealed, "My first time was a disaster. The boy was like me, no experience. I was in pain for days." She shook her whole body, exaggerating the memory of her pain.

"God, Emem, your mind is going far o!" I begged.

"Don't worry; the pain of the first time is worth the pleasures of a lifetime." She winked at me and rubbed her forefinger under my chin.

"You are rotten," I said before pushing her away and folding my arms across my breasts in horror.

"No, just real, my dear. And make sure he uses his raincoat o," she said as she pulled her ear. "The last thing you want is to get pregnant with Grandpapa," she added with a big cackle.

She turned to walk away, but I pulled her back. "Wait, that's another thing. How will I talk to him? He is a fine man, but he is old enough to be my father."

Emem burst out laughing again. "When he is rubbing your body, do you think he will be thinking about how old you are? If he wants you to act like his daughter, then he will not ask you to give him things that he cannot have from his daughter."

She held my hands and said seriously, "My dear, if you like him, go ahead and enjoy yourself. You only live once!" I stood glued to the spot as I watched her walk away.

I had not even stopped to consider whether I liked Admiral or not, much less thought of having sex with him or having him caress my body. He was a handsome old man, and I liked his smile, but apart from the fact that I saw him dote on his daughter, I had very little basis, if any at all, on which to form an opinion about his personality. He had been very warm and charming all the times we had met, and I was endeared by the fact that he had taken the trouble to look for me. In my mind, that made me special.

The following night, the security guard again came to call me for a visitor. I hurriedly made my way outside, and to my great disappointment, this time it was not a Mercedes-Benz parked outside but an old Honda Accord. I stopped and stood in place for about five minutes before inching forward to discover who was asking to see me. Admiral had asked his driver to come and pick me up, to where I did not know. However, Sisi was still awake, so I could not go anywhere. I asked the driver to tell Admiral that I could not leave the house.

Later that same night, the security guard came to call me again. It was already eleven o'clock, and I was in my bedroom. Pebbles hitting my window got my attention. I went out again, and this time it was Admiral. I entered the car and allowed myself to sink into the leather seat. "So, you didn't want to see me, ehn?" he queried, and pulled my head into his chest with a playful grip.

"No, sir. I just couldn't leave the house at that time. Madam George was still awake. Where would I tell her I was going?" I grumbled, and freed my head from his grip.

He folded his arms, leaned against the car door, and opened his mouth in amazement. "That's not what I was told. The driver said you insisted that if I didn't come myself, I could forget seeing you, so here I am."

"Ah, Admiral, I didn't say that o," I pleaded.

He moved closer and asked me seriously, "But are you happy I came?

"Yes, I am happy you came," I said, betraying very little emotion.

"Are you sure, or are you just saying so for peace's sake?" he teased.

"Yes, I am sure."

He stretched his neck to look towards the house, and asked, "So is Madam George asleep now?"

"Yes, she is," I assured him.

He lost his composure for a second and sounded like a young street boy. "All right, let's go for a drive, then."

Now I had to come clean with Esther, but not completely. I could not reveal the identity of the person I was going out with, but I told her that I was going for a drive with a friend of mine and begged her to cover for me if Sisi happened to get out of bed and look for me. Thankfully she agreed, though I noticed the inquiring look on her face, which I ignored.

I got back into the car for the drive and Admiral took my hand, caressing it, as he drove with one hand. He asked so many questions: what village I was from, if I was planning to go to university, what I wanted to study, how I wanted to live my life, the things that made me happy or sad, and even what kind of man I liked. I had difficulty answering some of his questions, especially the one about my taste in men. I answered many questions with "I don't know," or I just laughed. Sometimes I did both. My laughter was soothing, according to him. He added that, even if I was not going to answer his questions, at least he was making me laugh, which to him was a good sign.

After telling him when my birthday was, he informed me that most of the Capriconians he knew were very determined and knew how to get what they wanted. He added that, as if being a Capricorn was not enough, I was an only child and was probably spoiled and used to having my way; that meant he was in trouble. This he said clutching his chest in mock fear. He told me his daughter, Alaere, was born under the same sign, and she was a handful, but he was not worried, as he was used to dealing with my type. Alaere had given him many years of practice. His references to Alaere made me wish that my father was somewhere talking about me with the same affection, but I did not express my jealousy. I wondered if he would talk about her every time we were together since he was identifying the ways in which we were similar, but I did not dwell on it. Instead, I considered the fact that he was very attentive to Alaere and that I could maybe look forward to him showing me the same attention.

After grilling me for a while, he offered to answer any questions I might have for him, but I could form the questions only in my head. I could not ask him about his alleged girlfriends, or ask that he confirm or deny all the rumours about himself in the tabloids. Despite his familiarity,

I could not bring myself to forget he was an elder. Ordinarily I would not be sitting with him having any kind of conversation. I would not even be allowed to look him in the eye because that would be disrespectful, yet here he was, talking to me as if I were his age mate. That fact kept my head busy because a lot of the things I wanted to say, things I would have said without thinking had he been my age, I couldn't say for fear of being rude—or worse, insolent. I struggled with this even as Emem, my consultant, had told me that age and the expectations of elders were scarcely considered in these types of affairs.

We ended up in Admiral's house, which looked and felt so different than it had the day of the party. During the day, the huge compound had not looked so frightening; there were trees and many flowers to appreciate. The air was soaked with the scent from the Queen of the Night hedges he had all around the fence, but with the darkness lit by cold searchlights and without the crowd of people, the ghostly shadows took over the atmosphere. I could not wait to get into the warm safety of the house, even though I was not sure I was ready for what might happen indoors.

I sat in the living room downstairs, and Admiral went upstairs. It felt like the first time that I was seeing the living room, even though it was not. The majestic portraits of Admiral and his children looked down upon me, Alaere's eyes seemingly questioning my presence. There was a large profile of a ship, carved in wood on one side of the wall. There was an old anchor sitting on the floor in the opposite corner. I had barely noticed these and other furnishings in the living room on my first visit; the pictures were so imposing and Alaere's eyes were growing increasingly vicious.

Admiral came down wearing a *jalabia*. He offered to get me a drink, but when I opted for a Coke, we got into a little "argument." He insisted that I drink something stronger, an adult drink, and after much back-and-forth, we settled on Bailey's Irish Cream with a lot of ice for me, and Remy Martin for him.

Armed with our drinks, we moved to a smaller, adjoining room where Admiral turned on the stereo and spread himself out on a couch. I picked a lonely seat as far away from him as possible, but before I could perch myself upon it, he ordered me to come over and sit by him. He ignored my protests that there was not enough room for me. I got up and sat on the arm of the couch, by his head. In one very swift motion, he moved me from the arm onto a seat and rested his head comfortably on my lap. That was more than forty years of wooing experience on display.

We sat and talked, switching between English and Ijaw. Although he had been living in the city for many years, he used some Ijaw expressions that I did not even know. We discussed the village and the illusions that people in the village had about the city. We chatted about the way things were in Port Harcourt and debated Niger Delta issues, and I was shocked to hear his opinions regarding the oil companies. "Think about it, my dear, a man comes into your father's house. He has paid his rent to your father, and then, tomorrow, your brothers go to him to demand more money for rent. The man has an agreement with your father, not with you. If you feel he is not paying enough rent, then go to your father to review the rental agreement. I am a businessman; my main concern is to make profits—within the confines of the law, of course. There are certain things I will not do in my business because I have a conscience and a concern for my people, but imagine if I did not. My driving force would be the profits and what I can get away with under the law. In addition, until someone enforces it, what is the law but words on paper? That is the problem with the oil companies. The government that should be enforcing the laws to protect us in the Niger Delta is in fact putting our heads on the chopping block for the oil companies to finish the job. We, too, must take responsibility for some of our problems. See, that is why you must go to school and get your degree so that no one has an excuse not to give you an opportunity in life."

For me, everything was the oil companies' fault. Though I agreed with him to an extent, I also knew that, where I was coming from, he would have a hard time convincing people with his arguments and that even if he did, it would not bring the oil companies any sympathizers. Government was far away in Abuja; the oil companies and their pipes were in our backyards. More importantly, government had a heavy hand of justice. No one wanted to be the next Ken Saro-Wiwa, led to the gallows with plenty of years left before their God-given three-score and ten. No one saw the need for us to die like flies if our deaths were to be in vain. The oil companies, with the help of government forces, flexed their muscles once in a while, but overall, they were a closer target than government on which people could vent their anger.

Admiral and I talked until very late, when he dozed off. He was so handsome with his dimples and the sprinkles of grey in his hair. I felt a deep sense of longing for him, not because of the comfort Emem hinted at, which was money, but because I was hoping that the relationship would give me a taste of close paternal affection that I had never had.

At one point, in his sleep, he shifted and started kissing my stomach, and I stiffened like a log. Luckily, he turned his head and fell back into sleep. I was not ready for the physical part of the relationship, so I was happy he was too tired to try anything more. I was also tired, but I dared not sleep at his place; apart from the fact that I had to go to work, I did not want to have to explain my absence to Sisi in the morning.

I woke him up gently. "Admiral, I need to go home now."

"Sorry, dear, I am so tired. Too much work!" He jerked up and stood, stretching his hands towards the ceiling.

The drive home was silent, with only the noise from the breeze outside invading my thoughts. I was happy that he had not made any physical demands. I was not ready for it, but because I had gotten so enamoured by him, I had no doubt I would have gone along with whatever he initiated. So the more he delayed, the better it was for me. I could not deny that I enjoyed his company. He was so attentive and sweet, except sometimes he really sounded like an old headmaster, especially when he was expressing his views on the Niger Delta.

We reached Sisi's house, and before I got out of the car, Admiral leaned over and kissed me on the cheek. Then he reached under his seat and brought out a bundle of money, which he handed over to me. "For your running around." I was taken aback. I refused to take the money, but he insisted, so I thanked him and bolted out of his car.

I was embarrassed. I was not expecting him to give me money, at least not so soon and not without my asking. There was still a lot for me to learn about him. I knew eventually there would be sex and there would be more money, so I had to resolve quickly my conflict of taking money from him. I questioned and reasoned, and still I was not comfortable with the bundle of money I held in my hand. I gripped the notes so tightly that my hand began to hurt.

The security guard opened the gate for me and asked, "Auntie, you dey okay?" I mumbled an answer, handed the bundle of money to him, and said, "Thank you. I sabi say I don disturb you plenty dis night." Without another word, I hurried to the house and let myself in. It was the first time I had left Sisi's house without permission. My mother would not have tolerated that if she found out, and I knew I would be in very hot soup if Sisi found out. Guilt brought hot tears to my eyes and fear to my heart, which was beating so fast and hard, I thought it would jump out of my chest. I was involved in something I was not ready for, and although it was early enough to change my mind and opt out, I found myself drawn to Admiral like a fly to a gourd of palm wine. I liked him. The way he talked to me made me feel much older and very special. I felt tingles go up and down my spine when he put his head on my lap. I liked the fact that, even though the first thing on his mind might have been getting me into bed, he did not appear to be in any rush to do so. I wanted him to dote on me as I had seen him dote on Alaere. I had never lacked female affection from my mother, and now Lolo, but I had never experienced attentive, male affection, except my brief experience with Sergio. I felt as though I was about to experience that, and I was pleased with the prospect.

I dreamt of Admiral that night. My dreams were happy, although I do not remember exactly what they were about. However, as soon as I woke up and remembered the previous night's mischief, I became unhappy, worried, and tense. Sisi was in the dining room, eating her breakfast and giving some instructions to Esther. I felt so guilty I could not even look her in the eye when I greeted her, much less sit with her and read the newspapers as I did most mornings when I had not worked the night shift. I went into the kitchen and made myself some oats, but I could barely eat. Two spoonfuls were all I could manage to force down my throat, after which I stared at the bowl until the oats grew cold and hard. I was able to gulp down my tea and made myself a corned beef sandwich to take to work. I hoped my appetite would return.

Sisi looked at me with a worried expression, but she did not ask me any questions. As soon as she left the dining room to ready herself for the day, I tried to explain the previous night to Esther just in case she found out from the security man that I had been out until very late. Before I had finished my first sentence, she cut me off, claiming that she was not interested. She advised me to be very careful, because if Sisi caught me, I was on my own. She would not stick her neck out for me. So that was our understanding—she would not rat me out, but she would not stand up for me either. I was on my own.

I was morose at work that morning. Emem asked almost every five minutes what was wrong with me, despite my assurances that all was well. Finally, she dragged me into the ladies' room to squeeze out from me what had my face covered in sadness. My account of the night with

Admiral did not draw any compassion from Emem. Instead, she slapped the back of my head. "You had me thinking that someone was dead. Look, you will soon get over this feeling of guilt. Do not think you are Lolo. Lolo has a name. She is from old money. She can afford to sit on her high horse and pass judgment on people because she hasn't experienced hardship. Even then, I don't think she is totally innocent." She shook her head and flung her arms into the air. "She must have had one or two of these affairs. Get yourself together. Save your money. If you save enough, you won't have to worry about working to be comfortable when you are in university."

"But I don't have a problem with that. Sisi has promised to take care of my education," I chipped in.

Emem quickly dismissed me with, "Do you want to be asking Sisi for every little thing you need? You need your own cash, my dear."

I did not feel any less guilty about proceeding, in deceit of everyone around me, into a relationship with Admiral. However, I still could not wait to see Admiral again, to share jokes with him, argue about our people, and speak my mother tongue. I wished he would come to the hotel that day for a meeting, but he did not.

That night, I waited in the kitchen for the guard to bring me a message from my night visitor, but he never came. A day passed, two days, three, and I was crestfallen. Why hadn't Admiral come to see me in four days? Maybe he had decided I was too young for him. Perhaps he was seducing another girl somewhere and had forgotten all about me. I shared my angst with Emem, and she was convinced he was not through with me. He was a busy man and had probably been taken out of town on a business trip or maybe he was just using the age-old trick men use of withdrawing attention and making you long for it.

Despite Emem's opinion, I had just about given up on Admiral when, five days later, his driver appeared in the hotel. He walked up to the front desk and said he had a message for me. We went to a private corner, where he told me Admiral had sent him to find out what time my shift ended. He was to pick me up at the end of my shift to take me to Admiral's house, which was less than ten minutes away from the hotel. We arranged to meet in the parking lot when my shift was over.

I could not control my smile after I had spoken with the driver; I was grinning like a Cheshire cat that had caught a family of docile mice. Emem called me a silly, useless girl for stressing her with my woes and then melting so easily at the sight of Admiral's driver. She teased me, saying she could imagine how my temperature would rise when I saw Admiral later that day and predicted that day would be the last day she saw me as a virgin. She claimed I was exuding take-me vibes and that, no matter how tired or busy Admiral was, our meeting would not end with just a kiss, as it had the last time. It did not matter how much I protested, I could not convince her otherwise. "You better do it now, because if you keep it till you're too old, they'll have to use machines to open those legs," Emem advised.

That day, my shift felt a hundred days long. Suddenly, snails had taken over the hands of the clock. I could not wait to see Admiral. Excitement had taken over all my prior fears. Nothing could have spoiled the rest of my day. I half-listened as Emem gave me some quick notes on what to expect.

As soon as my shift ended, I rushed out to meet Admiral's driver. When we got to Admiral's house, he was not there. The driver took me into the house and told me to wait for Admiral in the upstairs living room. As I sat there waiting nervously for Admiral, the cook came up to ask me if I wanted to eat or drink something. I asked him to bring me a malt drink and sipped on that for almost an hour, despite it growing warmer and less delicious with each sip.

I heard Admiral's voice when he came into the house. He took his time coming to meet me upstairs. I had expected he would rush upstairs to see me, but he did not and that made me nervous. My stomach was in knots.

When he finally came upstairs, I greeted him with an icy *okoido*. He looked at me with a smile playing around his lips. “Ah, is that how you greet someone you haven’t seen in so many days?” I did not respond; I just looked at him defiantly. Then, even as he smiled, his voice was stern as he commanded me to get up and give him a hug. I obliged, a bag of butterflies letting loose in my stomach. I had missed him! My small frame got lost in his broad chest as he closed his arms around me. I felt warm and safe.

He took my hand and led me to his bedroom, where he asked me to make myself comfortable. He had to leave me for a couple of minutes to take care of some things with the driver. I sat at a desk by his window, looking out at the front yard, trying to ignore the roar of blood rushing pell-mell through my body. I was trying to relax, but, with the imposing bed invading my peripheral vision, it was impossible. Even with the air conditioner on, I felt the wetness of perspiration in my armpits. I felt warmth between my legs, and though I suspected my day had come, I did not know exactly what to expect—but I hoped that I would not end up in pain for days, as had been Emem’s experience. Whatever the case, I was just about ready to do it and get it over with.

Admiral returned to the room after about thirty minutes that seemed like hours. “So, did you miss me?”

I smiled coyly, playing with a curl in my hair.

“You haven’t shown me how much you missed me. I had to force you to give me a simple welcome hug,” he said. He was standing at the door, head cocked to one side and with a crooked smile.

“I missed you,” I responded with a little frustration creeping into my voice.

“And I am still waiting to see how much you missed me.”

I got up and went to give him a kiss on the cheek. I had to tiptoe to reach his cheek, but before I could plant the kiss, he took me by surprise and pulled me into his chest and planted his lips on mine. Next, I felt his soft lips on my neck, and then he lifted me up and placed me gently on his king-size bed. He was kissing my ears, my neck—slowly, exploring. His hands were in my hair, stroking, playing with curls. I did not know what to do in return, so I just lay there with my eyes closed, too shy to meet his eyes, if they were open.

It all felt very awkward as I fought the intruding sounds of my mother's disapproving voice, telling me not to spoil myself. Nevertheless, I reasoned that she was far away, and there was no way she could know that I had spoiled myself; at least I hoped that she would not be able to tell only by looking at me. With this consolation I gave up my virginity to Admiral.

He saw the tears in my eyes after he was done and laughed. "You're a woman now. Don't worry, it gets better." He rolled off me, and I looked at the spot of blood that marked my initiation into womanhood. He asked if I was okay, and I said I was. Admiral had taken my innocence, which I had given willingly and happily to him. I hoped it gave me a special place in his heart. I was more concerned about how he felt about me than how I felt about the whole experience and its implications.

We lay in silence as he stroked my stomach. Then he asked me what I had planned for the rest of the evening. I really did not have any plans, but I had to get home soon. He had to go to his office, so he got up and began to get ready. He told me I could stay until I was ready to leave and his driver would drop me off wherever I needed to go.

Uncomfortable in his room without him, I put my clothes on and left as soon as he was gone. It seemed too lonely without him, and I wanted to share what had just happened with someone. I could not share it with Lolo, so I had to wait until the next day to share with Emem. As I left his house that evening, it seemed that every eye that looked upon me could see that I had lost my innocence that day. I tried to walk as normally as I could, although how much I succeeded is uncertain. For days after, the experience stayed with me. I felt the slight discomfort from the invasion of my body by Admiral.

At work the next day, Emem greeted me with a knowing smile, telling me my eyes were dancing. She further embarrassed me by asking for details. She wanted to know everything—every word that was spoken, every move! I recounted every detail as she listened in fascination. She sounded upset only when I admitted that he did not use a raincoat as she had advised and promised to get me some birth control pills. I could get them from any pharmacy, she said, but she would get me the first few packets from her pharmacy to make sure I did not buy fakes.

I was in such awe of Admiral and was taken by the fact that a man of his place in society wanted to be with me. Things had gone so well, I did not want to spoil anything. I wanted to make him happy and hoped that in return I would experience the emotional comfort, attention, and protection that I had seen between him and Alaere.

Twelve

After our first sexual encounter, I did not see Admiral again for almost two weeks. Each day of those two weeks felt like two weeks in itself. I could not go to his house because if he was not there, I did not have a story about who I was, nor did I have a sensible message to leave with his domestic staff. I had not been to the house enough times to establish a relationship with any of them, and Admiral had not presented me as someone to be given preferential treatment. The protocol to get into the house of a man of his status, without his permission or invitation, was certain to be much more than I could handle without help.

I waited to receive a message from him and expected his driver every other day. I was torn and worried about the one-sidedness of the relationship. I had to decide that I was ready to deal with seeing him on his own terms and at his own time. But already I felt jealous of everything and everyone who had his attention. Alaere probably knew where he was. His business and political friends could reach him or go to his house more easily than I could. Even Emem could not help me with the way I was feeling. For her it was just a situation I had to deal with. I would have to adjust and not get too emotional, she counselled, but I could not help it. I wanted Admiral for more than money; I was yearning for an emotional bond with him.

Admiral surprised me by coming to the hotel himself. I arrived at work, and one of my colleagues informed me that an uncle of mine had come looking for me during the day. They had told him that I was on the night shift and would be there later in the day. The next morning, as I was getting ready to close my shift, one of the porters came in to tell me that a man was waiting for me in the parking lot. It was Admiral. I waited until my shift was over before I went to see him. I was angry and wanted to show that in my actions. I gave him a very stiff *okoido* and mumbled a response when he asked if I had plans for the rest of the day. He must have sensed that I was upset but he didn't acknowledge it. Instead he laughed and said, "Get into the car, my friend, before you start acting like a witch who can't find her broom." I hesitantly entered his car and turned my face to look out of the passenger-side window.

He was his usual jolly self as we drove to his house. I was quiet, keeping myself from laughing at his jokes and resisting all his attempts at a jocular reunion. When we got to his house, he led me upstairs to his bedroom and I stood by the door as I entered. He leaned into me, my back against the door, and stroked my hair.

"Why are you acting like this?" he asked softly, still stroking my hair.

I was silent. I rolled my eyes and turned away from him.

"I am sorry. You know I have to travel a lot for my business, and the way things are these days, we are really battling to make sure that the military does not continue to oppress us. It is a real battle o."

His words did not touch me. I felt nothing in my heart for his words, but the fact that he was trying to give me an explanation and the tone in his voice were reaching my inner vulnerability.

"It's not nice. You just took off, and you didn't tell me, and I don't even have a way to reach you," I sulked.

"But if you came here, they would have told you I had travelled.

Okay, from now on, if I know before I have to travel, I will let you know; otherwise, I will send you a message. Okay? Am I forgiven?"

I shook my head. "Promise me it won't happen again. I don't like it."

"I promise." He made the sign of the cross on his chest.

I felt such a strong emotional need for him that the memories of his tenderness and my longing for him erased all my anger. He pulled me close and kissed me before he carried me to the bed. We made love, and it was less painful the second time around, although he did some things that made me feel very self-conscious—I think I would have been satisfied just lying on my back with him on top of me. Even Emem's little talks had not prepared me for such adventurous positions.

Before he drove me home that day, he introduced me to his cook. "Ifiye, dis na my small friend Laye. Any time she come, even when I no dey house, keep her comfortable."

At the gate, he said to the security man, "My friend, you see dis face, make sure say you let her enter dis house any time she come."

As we got on the road, he looked at me and asked, "Is that better? Now you can come to the house and feel comfortable, even when I am not there. I have introduced you as a special guest to the house."

All I did was smile. I was happy. I felt what I wanted to be, special.

Admiral was out of town a lot, but when he was in town, I saw him when I wanted. Often we played cat-and-mouse games because of the visitors he entertained in the evenings. They kept very late nights, discussing politics and business, so when I arrived on such nights, I had to sneak into the house through the kitchen. There was a passageway that led to a back staircase up to Admiral's bedroom. I would slip through and go there. Some nights I would fall asleep before he had finished with his meeting, many of which ran late into the early morning hours; in fact, it was not unusual for them to end a meeting at three a.m.

I had to lie to everyone around me to keep up my relationship with Admiral. Besides Emem, there was no one I could talk to about the relationship. I never tried to bring up the subject with Lolo, because I could guess what the outcome would be.

Therefore, some weeks, I would lie to Sisi that I was on the night shift so that I could spend the night with Admiral. Other times I would be at his house with him in the afternoon and just tell Lolo that I was with Emem. Lolo did not like my friendship with Emem very much. She feared that Emem would corrupt me, but she also appreciated that I needed to have my own friends, so she tolerated our friendship. She did not know Emem, but she had seen her several times at the hotel and claimed that there was just something about her she did not like. "Her eyes are too open," she often said. Lolo was very worldly, but with things such as love and sex, she was very reserved. She did not discuss those things. She could talk all day about men and how useless they were and how they could not be trusted, but she could not talk about intimate details. She could not talk about the things she liked about her sexual relationship with Kamal. If I asked for advice, she would say, "You are too young. Wait till you get older." I was almost eighteen. It made me wonder at what age she had her first sexual experience with a man and at what age she thought I would be ready. Lolo adored Kamal. She had not had a serious boyfriend before Kamal, so she did not talk about anything or anyone but Kamal. In that way she was just as naïve as I was, though she played the experienced, big girl.

On my birthday, January 16, Sisi and Lolo organized a party for me. I invited Emem, and Damiete was there; the rest were Sisi and Lolo's friends, who I did not know, but since my birthday provided an excuse for a celebration, they all came. It was the first time I remember that my birthday was celebrated with a cake and a party. In the village, my mother made me feel extra special on my birthday by cooking something exceptional for me, excusing me from chores, and generally doing my bidding because it was my birthday, but not once do I remember having a cake with candles and a party. I appreciated all the trouble that Sisi and

Lolo had gone through to help me celebrate my birthday and was grateful to them. Finally, I was eighteen, and this birthday marked more freedom, more responsibility, and less supervision.

We partied until late that night, and I kept hoping that Admiral would remember it was my birthday and surprise me. I do not know how I expected him to justify being at my party, but I hoped that he would come up with something. I found out later that he had dropped off a present for me at the gate. I was ecstatic when I received the package of perfume with a note that read, "My dear, see me tomorrow for another toast to your birthday. I hope you like the present. Admiral." I wondered if he picked it out himself, but I perished the thought. He did not pick out every gift he gave to Alaere, but at least he remembered to have someone shop for a gift. Therefore, I did not mind if he had not picked this gift out by himself.

The next day after work, I practically ran to Admiral's house. He was there, thankfully, so my bated breath was not drawn out for too long. He said he had come by himself to drop off my gift and had hoped to see me, but when he saw the number of cars in Sisi's compound, he decided to just leave the gift with the security man at the gate. He also had a special gift for me that he had not left at the gate. Before he handed the gift to me, he gave me a long speech about how he wanted me to go to school because he could tell I was an intelligent girl and had a bright future ahead of me. He promised that he would take care of everything that I needed to be a success in life. It almost sounded like a separation speech. He was in one of his serious modes, and I felt very uncomfortable when he was that way. I liked when he was in his jovial mode, when things were lighthearted.

He asked me when my exams were and if I had started studying. I told him I had not started studying seriously, but I knew that the registration period for the exams was around the corner and the exams were just a few months away. At that time, I had only discussed signing up for intense exam preparation classes with Sisi, who was going to pay for them. I still had to ask Mr. Moses to work out a schedule that allowed me to attend the classes.

The day after my eighteenth birthday, Admiral handed me a check for seventy-five thousand naira. It was the largest amount of money anyone had given to me at once. It was my birthday gift, money I was to spend wisely, to keep me comfortable so that I could focus on my studies. I did not know how to thank him for the money, for the gesture. I could not even begin to imagine what I would spend the money on, as I had saved up a reasonable amount in my bank account.

I was sending money to my mother, but I could not send her too much at once so that she believed it was all coming from my salary or respectable work-related dealings. Though I was not with her, I was still very concerned about what she thought and continuously heard her voice in my head, especially when I felt guilty about something.

"Admiral, this is too much money," I protested.

"I don't want you to have any excuses for not passing your exams. I want you to focus on your studies and on passing your exams, then we'll worry about the rest," he insisted.

I owed it to myself to succeed in my exams, but now I also owed it to so many other people—my mother, Sisi, Lolo, and now Admiral. I felt like it was only a matter of time before I crashed. The streets from my village to where I was now had been paved with gold. No one was blessed with so much luck. Even I, who had been blessed with so much in less than a year in Port Harcourt, could not be foolish enough to believe that life was really like this. Whatever spirit I had to thank for all my luck, I thanked her and prayed that she would not turn her back on me. I believed it had to be a female spirit with a mother's compassion. And for that I had to be very careful not to offend her, because female spirits unleashed the worst punishments when they were offended.

I was spending less time with Lolo because every spare moment I had I wanted to spend with Admiral. My days were full before I started my relationship with Admiral, but then most of my time was spent with Lolo, or at least she knew where I was. I started lying to her and avoiding her. She suspected I had a boyfriend, and one day when I was with her in her bedroom, she asked when she was going to meet the boy who was keeping me occupied. I opened my mouth in shock; she had caught me off guard, not just by her question but also by the seriousness of her tone.

"I don't have a boyfriend," I managed to say after I had recovered from my shock.

"What is your boyfriend's name?" Lolo was very serious.

"I don't have a boyfriend," I blurted out, very embarrassed by the question.

"Don't lie to me. I know you have a boyfriend. I can tell. Besides, Sisi says she hardly sees you at home these days, and I have not been seeing you as frequently as before. If you don't want to tell me, that's fine, but I will find out, and he better not be some riffraff."

"I don't have a boyfriend," I insisted.

"Well, just don't let any boy distract you o! I hope all these times I don't see you, you are somewhere studying for your exams." She was not pushing the subject any further.

"Yes, ma," I responded cheekily.

"Don't pass and you'll see what I will do to you," she threatened as she tapped the back of my head. She said it with a smile, but I knew that she would give me hell if I did not do well in my exams. I also knew that if she wanted to, she could easily find out who I was having a relationship with, and that unsettled me.

Sisi was old and had made it clear from the beginning that she had no energy to chase me around, so Lolo took very seriously her duty to take care of me and what was best for my future. In fact, Sisi usually talked to Lolo to find out what I was up to, and as long as I was with Lolo, or Lolo approved of what I was doing, it was okay with her.

As long as I was able to dribble everyone to carry on my affair with Admiral, I did. For a while, I did not have the watchful eyes of Lolo on me. She had wanted to spend Valentine's Day with Kamal, and he had come up with an excuse why he could not be in Port Harcourt and why Lolo could not visit him in Lagos. She ignored him and went anyway; though I was not privy to the details, I knew things had not gone well during that visit. Shortly after that, Lolo took off to London for almost two weeks, and when she got back, it was even more apparent that things were not well between them. Lolo's hours had never been complete without at least three references to Kamal; then, suddenly, there was no talk of Kamal. It seemed everyone else was in on the secret because they didn't bring up his name either. I asked her one day about my brother-in-law, and she gruffly asked me not to spoil her day. She had become grumpy and withdrawn, spending more time at home than with Sisi or me.

Though I was at Admiral's house at least three days a week, I was not seeing him that often. He was increasingly occupied by politics, and there were so many demands on his time. I remember one evening I went to his home after work and found at least twenty young men milling around the house. I could see some of them were injured. Others just looked roughed up—shirts unbuttoned, trousers dirty, and just generally dishevelled. I asked the cook, Ifiye, what was going on, and he explained to me that there had been ethnic clashes in Warri and that these boys had come to ask for financial support from Admiral. They could have sent one or two representatives, I reasoned. Admiral was not home.

"No mind dem; na so dem dey do. Dem no sabi do anytin wit sense," Ifiye responded to my questioning eyes.

I went up to Admiral's bedroom and studied until I fell asleep. The usual practice was that if I fell asleep before he was done with his meetings, he would wake me up when he got into bed. He did not always intend to wake me up but usually the desire to see him was so strong that I could will myself to stay somewhere between consciousness and oblivion. Unless I was extremely tired, I woke up as soon as he crept into bed.

The next morning I woke up, and it did not look like Admiral had come to bed. I took a bath, got dressed, and prepared to leave. By the time I reached the top of the stairs, I could hear voices. The young men were still there! Admiral was sitting in his chair, holding his head with one hand and listening to them tell their tales of battle.

They needed money to pay the hospital bills of some of their friends who had been injured and money to bail out others who had been detained by the police. Admiral gave them the money but was also worried about the implications of another Ijaw/Itsekiri clash in Warri.

"They are the ones starting the trouble, so we have to defend ourselves, sir."

Each time there was a clash, the Itsekiris were the first to cry foul and report in the press that the vicious, heartless Ijaws had killed hundreds of their kin. In return, the Ijaws would report that they were going about their simple fishing lives when the Itsekiris started trouble and that the Itsekiris had massacred hundreds of their own kin. All is fair in love and war, they say, but the situation in Warri was worrisome. Each side claimed they were the victims of the other's barbaric tendencies. So many people of mixed Ijaw and Itsekiri parentage had been killed in the conflicts. It was all just senseless.

I had heard enough debates played out in that same living room about the Itsekiri and Ijaw conflict in Warri. Who owned the land? Who were the tenants? Who deceived whom? In what year? Answering all of those questions still did not provide a solution that was acceptable to both sides, so I did not care, particularly on that day. I just wanted to see Admiral and was quite upset that I had not gotten to see him or feel him that day.

The so-called youth groups had become well oiled extortion machines all in the name of the struggle. They stole, blackmailed, and vandalised for the progress and development of the Ijaw Nation, the Niger Delta. Some days I appreciated their efforts—bringing focus on the suffering of the Niger Delta people—but I could not help but feel that they were holding ransom one of their own. If Admiral did not give them money, then he was not doing anything for the Ijaw Nation—at least that would be their version of the story. Their story would not include the fact that he did not want to encourage violence as the first line of action, or that he wanted the youths to engage the oil companies and the government positively. No. They would exclude all of that from the reports. Therefore, that day, I was very unappreciative of their existence.

There would be more days like that. Days when I would be so close to Admiral, in his house, but unable to see him, or if I did see him, it was for five to ten minutes because he was discussing politics in his living room. Days when he would meet me in his bedroom, hastily ask how I was doing, and put a wad of money in my handbag so that he could return to the discussions in his living room. They talked about how the oil companies were using the Nigerian armed forces as their private security details to terrorise and sometimes kill innocent villagers who questioned the inequity of their situation—living in squalor while barrels of oil pumped out of their land provided the luxury that surrounded the oil workers and the elite of Nigeria. They held heated debates about which Ijaw man had disappointed the entire group as a people by his nonperformance in a position of political or economic power. There were discussions about who would be suitable candidates for political power if and when the opportunity came, and more talk about how to move the Ijaw Nation forward, economically and socially. Yes, these discussions were important, but what was more important to me was to have Admiral's undivided attention.

As my exam date got closer, I put all my energy and the pieces of my heart into my studies. I had not given myself much time to study for the exams, so I just crammed. I lived on my books. Sleep and hunger stayed away from me as if conspiring and then deciding to be part of the emotional torture I was enduring.

By late March, only days away from my exams, my body had given up. I was dragging myself around. My eyes were swollen and red, my skin was pale, and my lips were red from my nervous biting. Mr. Moses kindly gave me time off work until I finished my exams. Sisi and Lolo were worried and ordered me to rest. They took away my books one weekend, forced me to eat, and gave me Valium to help me sleep.

I was so lost in my own world that I did not notice the fanfare for the Pope's visit to Nigeria. There were special masses, meetings in Abuja, prayers, and so on. Even the head of state, who was making very limited public appearances, made an appearance for the Pope.

Physically I was in poor shape, but I managed to write all my exams. By the time it was over, I was feeling more relaxed but still very tired. Sisi took me to her doctor, and without a physical exam, he stated that my body was just reacting to the stress under which I had put it. He gave me some iron tablets for my anaemia and Vitamin B complex for energy. He promised that in no time I would feel better.

One can say sickness or wellness is in the mind, so when I was able to see Admiral, I felt very good. I knew he was busy, but I could not help but wonder if he had moved on to another young girl. After all, he did have a reputation for liking very young girls. I had not heard anything, but since nothing had leaked to the tabloids about his affair with me, I was not comforted.

Emem tried to convince me that I was being morose where there was no need to be. I had to understand that Admiral was a busy man. He was good to me when he saw me, so I should be grateful for that. I shared my concern that I might be pregnant, because I had not been feeling well and my menstrual period was very late. She chucked it up to stress and carelessly said that if I was pregnant, it was not the end of the world and she could help me deal with it if necessary. I was inclined to accept stress as the cause of my delayed period. Apart from the fact that I occasionally felt lethargic, I did not have the morning sickness or dizziness that I had heard so much about.

I wished I could talk to Lolo, but she was going through her own issues with Kamal. Whatever it was, no one talked about it, but everyone knew that Lolo and Kamal were on the outs. In my eyes, they had the perfect relationship, so I could not even venture a guess as to what their problems were. Moreover, Lolo left very little room for intrusion because she was rarely in town. She shuttled between London and Port Harcourt as if she were going from Port Harcourt to Buguma. The only person who seemed happy about the situation was Pa, Lolo's father, who was just happy because it meant there was a chance for his friend, Damiete, to pick up the reins Kamal had dropped.

I did not know what to do, and I needed someone to talk to. I had failed in a major way, and I had to make it good without losing face. Emem had been a good confidant up until that point, but I wanted to share this problem with Lolo. She could beat me up and still comfort me with the same hands—the hands of a sister who cared for me. I did not think I could get the same intimacy from Emem.

When I was finally able to talk to Admiral, I was almost certain. I could not explain what was different, but I felt different; my insides felt different. I was sitting on his bed, and he was reading some documents at his desk.

"Admiral, I am pregnant." The words rushed out as though they would choke me if I said them any slower.

He did not even raise his head from his paper. "Hmm, how do you know you are pregnant?"

"I just know," I said, frustrated.

"Have you gone to see a doctor?" he asked halfheartedly, still reading his paper.

"No, but I know I am pregnant." The tone of my voice was rising, exposing my exasperation.

I stood up and went to put my hands on his shoulders. "Admiral, are you even listening to me?"

He stopped reading and sat me on his lap. "I heard you. You say you are pregnant, not so?"

"Yes, so what am I going to do?"

"Well, first you have to confirm that you are pregnant, and only a doctor can do that. And if you are pregnant, I have a friend who can take care of it."

Then with the same absentmindedness with which he had been listening to me, he said, "Please let me finish this and then we can talk, okay?"

I had expected a warmer response from him. Instead, he was cold and distant, like he did not care. I felt as if I had been gutted, and for the first time since I suspected the pregnancy, I felt the urge to vomit. I quickly packed up my things, forced out a good-bye to Admiral, and dashed out of his house. He barely looked up to say good-bye.

A few days later, Sisi's security guard called for me late in the night. It was Admiral waiting for me outside the gate. It had become common practice for the security man to call me out at night to see Admiral or his driver; because I rewarded him handsomely, he did me the favour of announcing their presence with the utmost discretion. Esther also got her rewards for zipping her lips about my late-night escapades. Although she rarely accepted cash from me, she accepted the little gifts that I got for her when I went to the market.

"Why did you run off the other day?"

"I didn't run off. You were busy, so I left," I hissed.

"So have you gone to see a doctor?"

"No, but I'll go this week," I said hurriedly.

"Well, take this," he said, and handed me an envelop full of money. "Go to Island Clinic and ask for Dr. George. Tell him you need a pregnancy test, and if you are pregnant, he will help you get rid of it."

I looked at him, and I could not find any softness in his face. His boyish countenance with the dimples looked more like a frightening apparition. I almost choked on a scream as I tried to smother it. Since I could not shout, I wanted to at least smash all the windows in his car. I was allowed a tantrum for his callousness.

There was no room for a discussion. He did not ask whether I wanted to keep the child or not. He did not care, and if I kept the baby, I was definitely on my own. Sisi would undoubtedly send me packing. She had signed on to help enable me to further my education, not start a family.

I was jolted into reality. Admiral did not have the time to commit to me, and expecting anything more from him was stupid. In my romanticised view of Admiral, he would hold me, tell me he could not wait to receive the product of our love, and even propose to marry me. Why not? There were tons of older men who had married young girls who found a balance between having their babies with studying for their final exams and eventually writing their thesis for doctorate degrees. Even if he did not propose, he would give me assurances that there was no need to panic because he would take care of me. I expected that a man his age, with his comforts, would welcome the news of fathering a child. But I should have known better, and I had no one to blame but myself since his reputation with young girls far, far, preceded him.

Dr. George was out of the question. He had to be the doctor who rich men sent their girlfriends to for abortions. Admiral had probably sent dozens of girls to him. I could not bear the shame of being seen as one of the poor little girls taken advantage of by her sugar daddy. Admiral would have discussed the situation with Dr. George, and one indiscreet nurse meant that my story would be all over town. I could not risk that.

A pregnancy test kit from a pharmacy confirmed that I was pregnant, and then another reality surfaced—there was a possibility that the seed growing in my stomach was not planted by Admiral.

Thirteen

I had gone to Lolo's bank to make a deposit for her. After I finished the transaction, I had some time to kill before my shift that afternoon. I was a short distance away from the bank when I heard fast footsteps behind me. I looked back and saw a young man running towards me. I made way and shifted towards the dirt side of the road so that he could run past me. But as I turned, he slowed down.

"Sister, sister, na you I dey try catch," he said, panting.

"Na wetin?" I asked slowly, trying to hide my amusement.

"My oga say make I call you."

"Who be your oga?" I asked impatiently.

He turned and pointed towards the bank, to a white man who was standing in front of a white pickup truck. I stood for a few minutes, looking at the white man beckoning to me and at the poor young man who had been sent to chase me down. I stood for a moment, trying to decide if I wanted to speak to this whitey.

Even after I met Sergio, I never put a colour to the man who would rescue me from my village existence. In fact, when I allowed myself to think about it, I thought it safer to keep away from white men just in case I committed a taboo with the father I had never known.

When I got to Port Harcourt, most of the young girls who were looking to escape their poverty were looking to white men to rescue them.

Every night, girls trooped into the hotel lobby, looking for a chance to snatch up a white man. Hundreds of girls left their villages to go to places like Warri or Bonny, to get their chance with a whitey. Though I was financially comfortable and somewhat emotionally fulfilled with Admiral, I was still very curious about what the mystique was with white men. Therefore, I looked at the poor young man and decided that, for his efforts—and to satisfy my curiosity, of course—I would follow him to meet his boss. Nevertheless, before we left, I had to feign resistance.

"What does he want?" I demanded brusquely.

"Abeg, I no sabi. De man just say make I call you. E be like say de man sabi you sef," he pleaded, as if his life depended on me seeing his *oga*.

"Is he mad? Sabi me from where? Does he think I am a prostitute that he can just call off the streets like that?"

"Ah, no o, sister, no be like dat at all. E be like say e sabi you, dat's all."

"I really don't have time for this. He better not waste my time with rubbish talk."

I moved towards the white man, wondering why he was grinning like a lucky fisherman meeting his new wife for the first time. Maybe because it was the last image I expected embodied in a chance meeting on the streets of Port Harcourt. The identity of the person before me did not instantly register in my brain. As soon as I recognised Sergio, I wanted to turn around and run. My stomach was tight from anger and excitement, but I managed to hide both. I had told myself plenty of times that he didn't owe me that last meeting and that I had no right to feel like a jilted lover; but all that self-affirmation didn't help me as I stood in front of him, wondering what to do and how to react. My shock was squeezed out of me with a tight hug from him.

"So good to see you. You look so different I almost didn't think it was you," he said in his mechanical, accented voice.

"Good to see you, too," I responded coolly. He was expressing enough excitement for ten people.

"I didn't expect to see you in Port Harcourt. Have you started school?"

"No, but I plan to start soon," I said.

"What are you doing now? Who are you staying with? How is your mother? When did you come to Port Harcourt?" He asked so many questions, I wondered which one to answer first; then he added, "I was on my way to lunch. Let me take you out, and then we can talk," he offered.

I struggled to come up with an excuse, but he insisted, saying that he wanted to catch up with me.

A restaurant, or any other public place for that matter, was out of the question. I had not told anyone in Port Harcourt about Sergio. It was an experience I preferred remained in the village. I feared that Admiral had eyes all over town looking out for me, ready to report to him any misstep I took. Port Harcourt could be too small sometimes.

For example, I remember one afternoon I had gone to visit Admiral, and the first thing he asked me as I walked into his house was, "What was wrong with you the day before yesterday?"

I looked at him, puzzled. "Nothing."

"No, that's not true. Were you not at Mile Two yesterday?" He dared me to lie.

I was at Mile Two. I had gone to the market and was on my way to Sisi's shop. I was a little down that day, but it could have been the weather or the fact that I had to be at work later that day. By the time Admiral confronted me, I honestly could not remember if there had been anything in particular that had made me upset.

"Yes, I was, but how do you know I was at Mile Two?"

"I have eyes everywhere, my dear. So think about that when you want to misbehave," he said, laughing, but I did not share the humour in this all-seeing, all-knowing revelation. In fact, it was rather frightening.

He could have been driving past that area himself, or he could have had me followed. Whatever the case, I knew I had to be very careful about hopping around town with a man, and a white man at that.

Finally, after trying unsuccessfully to persuade me to eat at a restaurant with him, he invited me to his place. He was staying in a guesthouse in New GRA, close to the hotel—and dangerously close to Admiral's house. I was not sure if Admiral was out of town, so agreeing to follow Sergio to his place that day was like a small fish dancing close to a fisherman's net: with luck I could slip through and not get caught. I did not want to explain to anyone who Sergio was. Seeing what I saw at the hotel, even I had my own notions when I saw young girls with older white men in Port Harcourt.

When we reached the house, he asked the steward to prepare lunch for us. We sat in the living room and chatted. He was still doing business with Tarilabo, although they had not started the timber business. While I listened to him talk, I waited to feel the same excitement as when we were together in my village, but Admiral was on my mind. It was possible that Sergio knew him, and that made our meeting in his house even riskier.

Admittedly, when I was in the village, I believed Sergio was the key to the door that would lead to a world of opportunities and dreams fulfilled. However, I had been lucky in Port Harcourt. Through Pastor Ikechukwu, Sisi and Lolo had adopted me. I had a sugar daddy who at least provided me with emotional and material comfort for some time. I had more than I could ask for. In my eyes, with people like Sisi, Lolo, and Admiral in Port Harcourt, there was no need to learn the incredible tricks girls played just to hook a white man. I did not need Sergio in the same way anymore, yet I was a bit curious about what it would be like being with a white man.

There could have been something they offered besides money, that thing that my mother had fallen for. It was that thing I had been looking to key in to. I had wanted to understand what it was besides money that made beautiful twenty-year-old girls look at their short, fat, ugly fifty-eight-year-old white husbands with so much affection. Maybe then I could understand better or with less anger why there were more and more of my kind—"African-profits," "born-troways," "ashawo-pickins," "father-unknowns,"—running around the slums of Port Harcourt. Maybe then I would not hide from the facts of my birth that my yellow skin and curly hair put on display.

Unfortunately, and to my annoyance, I found it easy to get comfortable again with Sergio. I got lost in his voice, in his words, hearing nothing in detail, partly because half my brain was occupied by the question, "What happened to you that night?" We ate lunch accompanied by red wine and a million words from Sergio. All the while, I held myself back from asking why he had not shown up that night.

"I feel like I am doing all the talking. I don't remember you being this quiet," he said.

Then it fell out of me. "I waited for you that night. What happened?"

"Ah, I knew there was something wrong. I am so sorry about that day. After we got back from the forest, we went to see Tarilabo's friend in another village, and we were there until very late. We got back so late and left very early the next morning, I didn't want to disturb you."

"But you could have left a message with one of the people in the Semoke house. You just left like that, without saying anything, knowing that we had agreed to meet."

"I'm so sorry. I didn't think of that."

"You people never do."

"'You people'? Do not say that. I am really sorry, and you see, fate has given me another chance to make up for it."

"Really?"

"Yes, really. So, please, forgive me. I am sorry."

He stood up and reached out for my hand. "Let's go to the living room."

Still unsure about how the afternoon would end and what I wanted from him, I tried to flee while I still had my senses together. "I have to leave for work soon."

"Relax, you still have plenty of time. I will drop you off," he offered, and I didn't protest.

And so we got cosy on the sofa with our glasses of wine, listening to music.

He made the moves, kissing my ear and my neck, and I was turned on. My curiosity was getting the better of me. I wanted something to compare with Admiral since I'd only been with him. My curiosity, the kisses, the wine—it all went to my head and I followed Sergio's lead. We ended up making love, and although it felt different from being with Admiral, I could not say that physically I liked one over the other. Emotionally, I longed more for Admiral. Sergio took me to work that day, although I made him drop me a few metres from the gate.

I went back to see him a few more times but stopped because, although I enjoyed his company and the physical pleasure, it was difficult and dangerous lying and stealing time from other parts of my life to keep up our meetings. When I was with him, I had two fears—being caught by Admiral and that one day I would again wait endlessly for a promised meeting with him. Sergio had a family in Spain that he was sure to return to. He talked about them often and had shown me their pictures in his wallet, his beautiful wife and their twenty-year-old twin boys.

Sergio was a nice man, but I did not feel the same way for him as I felt for Admiral. I wanted someone who would understand my deepest emotions when I spoke in my mother's language, someone with whom I could feel protected and secure. I could not speak to Sergio's intentions because we never explored those issues, but I understood that we were from different worlds that would never meet, as I was not ready to let him into my world.

For my mother, even though she would never admit it negatively, I was a constant reminder of the man who broke her heart and gave her the gift of a child in its place. I do not know if she thought of my father with animosity or if she truly loved him, because she tried very hard not to speak of him.

I could not bring Sergio's child into my world. I could not allow him a place in my heart. That would have been foolish. He was a white man, and as far as I was concerned, his home was somewhere other than Nigeria; he was a transient white man with whom I had no future because as I had learnt, his type left when they had to—and without looking back. My views on the matter may have been tainted by my circumstances, but I would not say that I was angry. It was a situation in which I did not want to live or bring a child.

My mother was brave to have chosen to give me life over the pursuit of her dreams. I was not that brave. I could not deal with all the uncertainties. But I faced uncertainties regardless of whether Admiral or Sergio sired the child. Admiral had become distant, but I was not sure if it was because he had moved on to the next young girl. If he had, she must have been in Lagos or Abuja, because, increasingly, he was spending more time shuttling between Lagos and Abuja.

After he handed me the cash and referred me to Dr. George, I had not gone to look for Admiral and he had not tried to look for me, either. Those promises of "I will take care of whatever you need" were falling on the ears of another pretty young girl, another girl desperate for love or just in it for the money.

Admiral did not have to tell me he was not ready to have more children. He had two children who he took very good care of, and that was it. The other children he was interested in were the ones who kept his bed warm. I had benefited from Admiral, and my bank account was enough proof. For a few months, I had bonded with the man who initiated me into womanhood, and while the going was good, he had taught me a few lessons about how to survive in the world. The best thing to do was hang on to the pronouncement that he wanted me to succeed in life and to the pledge that he would do anything for my success, whether or not it was true.

I still intended to go to school. I had to do this for myself and for my mother. A child with no father was a sure way to throw my education out the window, because all the goodwill I had received from Sisi and Lolo was sure to be packed up with my suitcase, my baby, and me and sent expressly back to the village. I had seen babies halt young dreams; block golden opportunities; and change young, happy, carefree girls into grumpy, struggling mothers.

There were other people around me whose fathers were a mystery to them, just like mine was to me. Men who had strayed from their "happily" married lives and fathered some of them; men in high society who had no problem sleeping with their lower-class mothers but remembered their social status when they got someone pregnant.

Nevertheless, their secrets were not revealed in their complexion or the waves in their hair; mine was. With them, you could see their father's eyes, his forehead, his smile, but you had to look hard for it. I could not deal with trying to explain to my child that its father was a nice white man who offered me no security or maybe that its father was the man on network news every month discussing the Niger Delta.

I woke up one morning in June and walked to Lolo's house. I had not seen her in a couple of weeks and was not sure she was back from London, but I wanted to talk to someone. Someone I knew who cared. I wanted to confide in her. I missed her, and I missed our closeness, but I appreciated that she was going through her own issues. She still had not made up with Kamal, but Damiete wasted no time playing out his role as a caring friend.

When I reached her house, she was outside with Damiete and they were loading his pickup truck with jerry cans for petrol. Fuel was scarce again in Port Harcourt. A country from whose belly crude oil was lifted could boast of no working refineries, leaving us with incessant fuel scarcity.

Lolo received me well, like always. When I saw her, I knew I could not tell her about my pregnancy. I liked being little Laye in her eyes. I liked the way she put her arms around my shoulders, bringing me close to her. I missed her scent, so sweet and mellow, like a bouquet of flowers. She looked happy to see me and asked how I was and whether my exam results were out. She was happy to see that I had put on some weight since almost killing myself studying for the exams. I asked how she was, and she said she was okay. She did not say much more, and I could not ask. I was the younger one; prying would have been rude. She invited me to go with them to the filling station to buy petrol.

When we got to the filling station, there was a guarded excitement in the air besides the regular commotion around the long queue for petrol. People were whispering in huddles. Some left their huddles laughing; some left mournful, shaking their heads as if in disbelief; some got on their knees and looked to the heavens. All that drama! Damiete left Lolo and me in the car and approached one of the huddles. After a few minutes, he returned to inform us that our head of state had died overnight. They had not made any announcements, but news had filtered to the Nigerian people.

We filled our jerry cans and returned to Lolo's house. Lolo and Damiete were going to stay with Ma and Pa for the day until they knew what was going on and determined that there was no danger to worry about. I decided to go home, and Lolo allowed me to do so only after promising her that I was going straight to Sisi's.

I spent most of the day sleeping, and by the time I woke up that evening, it was like a carnival in the streets. People were dancing and jubilating over the death of the land's leader. I went downstairs, and Esther gave me the details she had gathered—the talk in the streets was that he had died of a heart attack after taking a drug to enhance his performance with two Indian prostitutes. There was no rioting, she reported, just people celebrating the demise of a villain. A divine power had acted on behalf of the people—God, Allah, and all our spirits, had heard the collective prayers of Nigerians. That is what people were saying.

I decided to go out to see things for myself. I walked to the kiosk around the house where a few people had gathered and were, as expected, soapboxing about Nigeria's future. There were speculations as to whether they would release from prison the winner of the last presidential elections to take his rightful place in power. Some were convinced another khaki-uniformed person would take over, and a few just did not care. What was indisputable was the excitement in the air. People breathed as they had not breathed in a long time. They talked about tomorrow as if they really believed in it, as though magically all the problems in their lives would be fixed tomorrow.

I left the kiosk and started strolling in no particular direction, hoping a long walk would give me a chance to think about my situation, make some decisions, and clear my head. The streets got quieter as my thoughts collided with each other.

Then one thought suppressed all others—I could take care of my problem myself, cover my shame, and look forward to my own tomorrow with a clean slate. I soon started looking for plants that resembled the ones girls in the village claimed were used to "wash out" *belle*. Old GRA houses were surrounded by all kinds of trees and plants, some growing wild along people's fences, and I had seen a few that looked like the acclaimed ones for washing out *belle*. I walked along Sisi's street and plucked a handful of every plant that corresponded with what my memory had recorded of the plant I needed. I prayed that I had not picked up anything lethally toxic. However, I was so determined to do something drastic that whatever the outcome of my potion, it had to be that day. I could not go on with my secret growing and every day threatening to expose my indiscretions.

I returned to my room later and chewed up the plants I had picked, leaf and bark together. Some were so bitter I had to force them down with water. The bitterness did not matter much as I willed myself to swallow and hold down every substance that I chewed out of the plants. I did not know what to expect, what I would feel, or if I would live to see the next day. However, if I lived, it was an opportunity for a personal rebirth along with Nigeria. I promised God and myself that I would focus only on completing my education and making my mother, Sisi, and Lolo proud of me. As much as I enjoyed the drama of working at the hotel, I knew in my heart that it was not what I wanted to do with the rest of my life. I wanted the confidence that Lolo had, and if Sisi was right, the choices also that came with an education.

Emem possessed a lack of seriousness that I did not envy, and she thrived on the kind of chaos that I could only appreciate from a distance. I knew that if I was around it long enough without my own focus, I could be sucked into it. My life was out of focus, and I wished for the days when my mother planned my life, but I could not go back to what I had rejected. I needed to refocus, and this time I would have to do it myself. Everything I had had in life up until that point had been handed to me on a platter, and I had taken it all for granted. I had forgotten the coarseness of my mother's hands, which worked tirelessly so that I could achieve more than she did. I had forgotten the friends I left behind to struggle for every meal. That evening I remembered. I saw my mother's face, and though there was very little

I had done in Port Harcourt that would have made her happy, she was smiling. I cried because through her smile I could hear her say that I had let her down. My chest grew tighter and tighter as I sobbed into my pillow, and fear and shame closed in on me until I felt suffocated. I sucked in huge doses of air, hoping to release the tightness in my chest, but all that did was make me dizzy. My fingers and toes went numb, and at some point, I feared that I might die. I cried but could not feel sorry for myself because I had made the choices that got me into trouble. I had allowed myself, like an empty canoe, to drift along with the flow of the river.

I felt near the end when the cramps woke me up later that night. I do not know for how long I lay in bed, unable to move because my legs refused to yield to my will, until somehow I managed to crawl to the bathroom. I lay curled up in the foetal position on the cold tile floor until my sweat and the blood that gushed from between my legs drenched my clothes, and I began to shiver from the cold and the pain. I begged God for forgiveness and called on all my mother spirits for comfort. Even so, I had to bite down on a towel to keep from screaming as my body pushed out blood and clumps of tissue that had been forming a little person inside me for almost three months. The pain stiffened my joints, and the smell of blood stormed my nostrils as my being drifted into a river. I could hear the waves slowly chasing after each other; some lapped over my stomach, while others collided with canoes at the shore. I was enveloped in darkness and kept company only by the sounds of the night that lulled me to sleep.

At daybreak when I awoke on the bathroom floor, I was grateful to see another day; that was luxury enough. The rest I would have to figure out.

Acknowledgments

I owe this effort to Ken Saro-Wiwa whose book *A Month and a Day: A Detention Diary* inspired me to write fiction. Thank you to all my friends and family who supported me through this entire process, especially "Rumbz," for the time, effort, and sincerity she gave to reading and editing my first draft, and my cousin Efere, who dragged me across the finish line with his many lectures.